Faces in the Water

Also by Janet Frame

Novels

Stories and Sketches

Poetry

Janet Frame

FACES
IN
THE
WATER

GEORGE BRAZILLER

NEW YORK

For information address the publisher:
George Braziller, Inc.
One Park Avenue
New York, NY 10016

Library of Congress Cataloging in Publication Data
Frame, Janet.
  Faces in the water.

  I. Title.
PZ4.F812Fac   1980   [PR9639.3.F7]   823   79-25441
ISBN 0-8076-0957-9

Paperback reprint edition 1982 by George Braziller, Inc.
Printed in the United States of America

        Grateful acknowledgment is made for permissions received from
the following copyright proprietors:
Sidgwick & Jackson Ltd., for the lines on page 25, from "Moonlit Apples"
from *The Collected Poems of John Drinkwater.*
Leo Feist, Inc., for the lines on page 48, from "Rainbow on the River."
Lyric by Paul Francis Webster. Music by Louis Alter. © Copyright 1936
by Leo Feist, Inc., New York, N. Y.
Random House, Inc., for the lines on page 118, from the poem "Lauds"
by W. H. Auden.
Jonathan Cape Limited and Mrs. H. M. Davies, for the lines on page 160,
from *The Collected Poems of W. H. Davies.*
W. W. Norton Company, Inc., for the lines on page 161, from *Sonnets
to Orpheus* by Rainer Maria Rilke, translated by M. D. Herter Norton.
Copyright, 1942, by W. W. Norton & Company, Inc., New York, N. Y.
Joy Music, Inc., for the lines on page 179, from "My Dreams Are Getting
Better All the Time." Lyric by Mann Curtis. Music by Vic Mizzy. Copy-
right 1944 by Joy Music, Inc., N. Y.
Charles Scribner's Sons, for the lines on page 183, from "Never Get Out,"
from *The Collected Poems of John Galsworthy.* Copyright 1934 by Charles
Scribner's Sons.
Williamson Music, Inc., New York, N. Y., publisher and owner of publica-
tion and allied rights to "Some Enchanted Evening," for the lines from
that lyric on page 199. Copyright © 1949 by Richard Rodgers and Oscar
Hammerstein II.

To. R. H. C.

PART ONE

Cliffhaven

I

*T*HEY HAVE SAID that we owe allegiance to Safety, that he is our Red Cross who will provide us with ointment and bandages for our wounds and remove the foreign ideas the glass beads of fantasy the bent hairpins of unreason embedded in our minds. On all the doors which lead to and from the world they have posted warning notices and lists of safety measures to be taken in extreme emergency. Lightning, isolation in the snows of the Antarctic, snake bite, riots, earthquakes. Never sleep in the snow. Hide the scissors. Beware of strangers. Lost in a foreign land take your time from the sun and your position from the creeks flowing towards the sea. Don't struggle if you would be rescued from drowning. Suck the snake bite from the wound. When the earth opens and the chimneys topple, run out underneath the sky. But for the final day of destruction when "those that look from the windows shall be darkened" they have provided no slogan. The streets throng with people who panic, looking to the left and the right, covering the scissors, sucking poison from a wound they cannot find, judging their time from the sun's position in the sky when the sun itself has melted and

9

trickles down the ridges of darkness into the hollows of evaporated seas.

Until that day how can we find our path in sleep and dreams and preserve ourselves from their dangerous reality of lightning snakes traffic germs riot earthquakes blizzard and dirt when lice creep like riddles through our minds? Quick, where is the Red Cross God with the ointment and plaster the needle and thread and the clean linen bandages to mummify our festering dreams? Safety First.

I will write about the season of peril. I was put in hospital because a great gap opened in the ice floe between myself and the other people whom I watched, with their world, drifting away through a violet-colored sea where hammerhead sharks in tropical ease swam side by side with the seals and the polar bears. I was alone on the ice. A blizzard came and I grew numb and wanted to lie down and sleep and I would have done so had not the strangers arrived with scissors and cloth bags filled with lice and red-labeled bottles of poison, and other dangers which I had not realized before—mirrors, cloaks, corridors, furniture, square inches, bolted lengths of silence—plain and patterned, free samples of voices. And the strangers, without speaking, put up circular calico tents and camped with me, surrounding me with their merchandize of peril.

But I liked to eat Carmello chocolate because I was lonely. I bought twelve cushions for sixpence. I sat in the cemetery among the chrysanthemums bunched in their brownish water inside slime-coated jam jars. I walked up and down in the dark city, following the gleaming tram lines that held and arrowed the street lights and the trams flashed sudden sparks above my head and made it seem, with rainbow splashes of light, that I looked through tears. But the shopwindows were speaking to me, and the rain too, running down inside the window of the fish shop, and the clean moss and fern inside the florists, and the dowdy droopy two-piece sets and old-fashioned coats hung on the aged plaster models in the cheaper shops that could not afford to light their windows, and crowded their goods together, displayed with large warning tickets painted in red. They all spoke. They said Beware of the Sale, Beware of Bargain Prices. Beware of traffic and germs; if you find a handkerchief hold it up by the tip of the finger and thumb until it is claimed. For a cold in the chest be steamed with Friars' Balsam. Do not sit on the seat of a public lavatory. Danger. Power lines overhead.

I was not yet civilized; I traded my safety for the glass beads of fantasy.

I was a teacher. The headmaster followed me home, he divided his face and body into three in order to threaten me with triple peril, so that three headmasters followed me, one on each side and one at my heels. Once or twice I turned timidly and said, Would you like a star for good conduct? I sat all night in my room, cutting out stars from sheets of gold paper, pasting the stars on the wall and across the door of the landlady's best wardrobe and over the head and face and eyes of her innerspring divan, till the room was papered with stars, furnished as a private night, as a charm against the three headmasters who made me drink tea in sociability every morning in the staff room, and who tiptoed in sand shoes along the marigold border, sprouting pungent advice possibilities and platitudes. With my briberies for good conduct I fancied I held them fast with flour and water in a paper galaxy of approval, when I was really giving to myself alone the hundred rewards, guarantees, safety measures, insurance policies, because I alone was evil, I alone had been seen and heard, had spoken before I was spoken to, had bought fancy biscuits without being told to, and put them down on the wall.

My room stank with sanitary napkins. I did not know where to put them therefore I hid them in the drawer of the landlady's walnut dressing table, in the top drawer, the middle drawer and the bottom drawer; everywhere was the stench of dried blood, of stale food thrown from the shelves of an internal house that was without tenants or furniture or hope of future lease.

The headmaster flapped his wings; he was called a name that sounded like buzzard which gave him power over the dead, to pick the bones of those who lie in the desert.

I swallowed a stream of stars; it was easy; I slept a sleep of good work and conduct excellent.

Perhaps I could have dived into the violet sea and swum across to catch up with the drifting people of the world; yet I thought Safety First, Look to the Left and Look to the Right. The disappearing crowds of people waved their dirty handkerchiefs held, fastidiously, between thumb and forefinger. Such caution! They covered their mouth and nose when they sneezed, but their feet were bare and frozen, and I thought that perhaps they could not afford shoes or stockings, therefore I stayed on my ice floe, not willing to risk the danger of poverty, looking carefully to the left and the right, minding the terrible traffic across the lonely polar desert: until a man with golden hair said, "You need a rest from chrysanthemums and cemeteries and parallel tram lines running down to the sea. You need to escape from sand and lupines and wardrobes and fences. Mrs. Hogg will help you, Mrs. Hogg the Berkshire sow who has had her goiter out, and you should see the stream of cream that flows from the hole in her throat and hear the satisfactory whistling of her breath."

"You have made a mistake," Mrs. Hogg said, standing on tiptoe, her head thrust in the air. "I may have ginger whiskers but there has never been a stream of cream that flows from the hole in my throat. And tell me, what is the difference between geography, electricity, cold feet, a child born without wits and sitting drooling inside a red wooden engine in a concrete yard, and the lament of Guiderius and Aviragus,

> *Fear no more the heat o' the sun,*
> *Nor the furious winter's rages . . .*
>
> *No exorciser harm thee*
> *Nor no witchcraft charm thee.*
> *Ghost unlaid forbeare thee.*
> *Nothing ill come near thee."*

I was afraid of Mrs. Hogg. I could not tell her the difference. I shouted at her,

> Loony loony down the line,
> Mind your business and I'll mind mine.

What is a loony's business? A loony at Cliffhaven "down the line" where the train stops for twenty minutes to put down and collect the mailbags and to give the travelers a free look at the loonies gathered about, gaping and absorbed?

Tell me, what is the time now? The light-headed school bell is giddily knocking its head against its tongue; am I at school in time? The cherry blossom is budding in its burnished leaves, the velvet-tonsiled snapdragons are in flower, the wind is brushing sunlight into the row of green supple poplars growing outside on the bank, just up the path. I can see them from the windows open only six inches at the bottom and the top, and why are the doors locked by people who wear pink uniforms and carry keys fastened by a knotted cord to their belts and kept inside deep marsupial pockets? Is it after teatime? Violet light, yellow japonica, the children in the street playing hopscotch baseball and marbles until the blotting darkness absorbs even the color from the yellow japonica?

I will put warm woolen socks on the feet of the people in the other world; but I dream and cannot wake, and I am cast over the cliff and hang there by two fingers that are danced and trampled on by the Giant Unreality.

So there was nothing to do but weep. I cried for the snow to melt and the powerful councilors to come and tear down the warning notices, and I never answered Mrs. Hogg to tell her the difference for I knew only the similarity that grew with it; the difference dispersed in the air and withered, leaving the fruit of similarity, like a catkin that reveals the hazelnut.

II

I WAS COLD. I tried to find a pair of long woolen ward socks to keep my feet warm in order that I should not die under the new treatment, electric shock therapy, and have my body sneaked out the back way to the mortuary. Every morning I woke in dread, waiting for the day nurse to go on her rounds and announce from the list of names in her hand whether or not I was for shock treatment, the new and fashionable means of quieting people and of making them realize that orders are to be obeyed and floors are to be polished without anyone protesting and faces are made to be fixed into smiles and weeping is a crime. Waiting in the early morning, in the black-capped frosted hours, was like waiting for the pronouncement of a death sentence.

I tried to remember the incidents of the day before. Had I wept? Had I refused to obey an order from one of the nurses? Or, becoming upset at the sight of a very ill patient, had I panicked, and tried to escape? Had a nurse threatened, "If you don't take care you'll be for treatment tomorrow?" Day after day I spent the time scanning the faces of the staff as carefully as if they were radar screens which might reveal the approach of the fate that had been prepared for me. I was cunning. "Let me mop the office," I pleaded. "Let me mop the office in the evenings, for by evening the film of germs has settled on your office furniture and report books, and if the danger is not removed you might fall prey to disease which means disquietude and fingerprints and a sewn shroud of cheap cotton."

So I mopped the office, as a precaution, and sneaked across to the sister's desk and glanced quickly at the open report book and the list of names for treatment the next morning. One time I read my name there, Istina Mavet. What had I done? I hadn't cried or spoken out of turn or refused to work the bumper with the polishing rag under it or to help set the tables for tea, or to carry out the overflowing pig-tin to the side door. There was obviously a crime which was unknown to me, which I had not included in my list because I could not track it with the swinging spotlight of my mind to the dark hinterland of unconsciousness. I knew then that I would have to be careful. I would have to wear gloves, to leave no trace when I burgled the crammed house of feeling and took for my own use exuberance depression suspicion terror.

As we watched the day nurse moving from one patient to another with the list in her hand our sick dread became more intense.

"You're for treatment. No breakfast for you. Keep on your nightgown and dressing gown and take your teeth out."

We had to be careful, calm, controlled. If our forebodings were unwarranted we experienced a dizzy lightness and relief which, if carried too far, made us liable to be given emergency treatment. If our name appeared on the fateful list we had to try with all our might, at times unsucessfully, to subdue the rising panic. For there was no escape. Once the names were known all doors were scrupulously locked; we had to stay in the observation dormitory where the treatment was being held.

It was a time of listening—to the other patients walking along the corridor for breakfast; the silence as Sister Honey, her head bowed, her eyes watchfully open, said grace.

"For what you are about to receive the Lord make you truly thankful."

And then we heard the sudden cheerful clatter of spoons on porridge plates, the scraping of chairs, the disconcerted murmur at the end of the meal when the inevitably missing knife was being searched for while the sister warned sternly, "Let no one leave the table until the knife is found." Then further scraping and rustling following the sister's orders. "Rise, Ladies." Side doors being unlocked as the patients were ordered to their separate places of work. Laundry, Ladies. Sewing room, Ladies. Nurses' Home, Ladies. Then the pegging footsteps as the massive Matron Glass on her tiny blackshod feet approached down the corridor, unlocked the observation dormitory and stood surveying us, with a query to the nurse, like a stockman appraising head of cattle waiting in the saleyards to go by truck to the slaughterhouse. "They're all here? Make sure they have nothing to eat." We stood in small groups, waiting; or crouched in a semi-circle around the great locked fireplace where a heap of dull coal smouldered sulkily; our hands on the blackened bars of the fireguard, to warm our nipped fingers.

For in spite of the snapdragons and the dusty millers and the cherry blossoms, it was always winter. And it was always our season of peril: Electricity, the peril the wind sings to in the wires on a gray day. Time after time I thought, What safety measures must I apply to protect myself against electricity? And I listed the emergencies— lightning, riots, earthquakes, and the measures provided for the world by man's Red Cross God Safety to whom we owe allegiance or die on the separated ice floe, in double loneliness. But it would not come to my mind what to do when I was threatened by electricity, except that I thought of my father's rubber hip boots that he used for fishing and that stood in the wash house where the moth-eaten coats hung behind the door, beside the pile of old Humor Magazines, the Finest Selections of the World's Wit, for reading in the lavatory. Where was the wash house and the old clothes with spiders' nests and wood lice in their folds? Lost in a foreign land, take your position from the creeks flowing towards the sea, and your time from the sun.

Yes, I was cunning. I remembered once a relationship between electricity and wetness, and on the excuse of going to the lavatory I filled the admission bath and climbed in, wearing my nightgown and dressing gown, and thinking, Now they will not give me treatment, and perhaps I may have a secret influence over the sleek cream-painted machine with its knobs and meters and lights.

Do you believe in a secret influence?

There had been occasions of delirious relief when the machine broke down and the doctor emerged, frustrated, from the treatment room, and Sister Honey made the welcome proclamation, "You can all get dressed. No treatment today."

But this day when I climbed in the bath the secret influence was absence, and I was given treatment, hurried into the room as the first patient, even before the noisy people from Ward Two, the disturbed ward, were brought in for "multiples," which means they were given two treatments and sometimes three, consecutively. These excited people in their red ward dressing gowns and long gray ward stockings and bunchy striped bloomers which some took care to display to us, were called by their Christian names or nicknames, Dizzy, Goldie, Dora. Sometimes they approached us and began to confide in us or touch our sleeves, reverently, as if we were indeed what we felt ourselves to be, a race apart from them. Were we not the "sensibly" ill who did not yet substitute animal noises for speech or fling our limbs in uncontrolled motion or dissolve into secret silent hilarity? And yet when the time of treatment came and they and we were ushered or dragged into the room at the end of the dormitory all of us whether from the disturbed ward or the "good" ward uttered the same kind of stifled choking scream when the electricity was turned on and we dropped into immediate lonely unconsciousness.

It was early in my dream. The tracks of time crossed and merged and with the head-on collision of hours a fire broke out blackening the vegetation that sprouts a green memory along the side of the track. I took a thimbleful of water distilled from the sea and tried to extinguish the fire. I waved a small green flag in the face of the oncoming hours and they passed through the scarred countryside to their destination and as the faces peered from the window at me I saw they were the faces of the people awaiting shock treatment. There was Miss Caddick, Caddie, they called her, bickering and suspicious, not knowing that she would soon die and her body be sneaked out the back way to the mortuary. And there was my own face staring from the carriageful of the nicknamed people in their ward clothes, striped smocks and gray woolen jerseys. What did it mean?

I was so afraid. When I first came to Cliffhaven and walked into the dayroom and saw the people sitting and staring, I thought, as a passerby in the street thinks when he sees someone staring into the sky, If I look up too, I will see it. And I looked but I did not see it. And the staring was not, as it is in the streets, an occasion for crowds who share the spectacle; it was an occasion of loneliness, of vision on a closed, private circuit.

And it is still winter. Why is it winter when the cherry blossom is in flower? I have been here in Cliffhaven for years now. How can I get to school by nine o'clock if I am trapped in the observation dormitory waiting for E.S.T.? It is such a long way to go to school, down Eden Street past Ribble Street and Dee Street past the doctor's house and their little girl's dollhouse standing on the lawn. I wish I had a dollhouse; I wish I could make myself small and live inside it, curled up in a matchbox with satin bed curtains and gold stars painted on the striking side, for good conduct.

There is no escape. Soon it will be time for E.S.T. Through the veranda windows I can see the nurses returning from second breakfast, and the sight of them walking in twos and threes past the border of snapdragons granny's bonnets and the cherry blossom tree brings a sick feeling of despair and finality. I feel like a child who has been forced to eat a strange food in a strange house and who must spend the night there in a strange room with a different smell in the bedclothes and different borders on the blankets, and waken in the morning to the sight of a different and terrifying landscape from the window.

The nurses enter the dormitory. They collect false teeth from the treatment patients, plunging them in water in old cracked cups and writing the names on the outside in pale blue ink from a ballpoint pen; the ink slips on the impenetrable china surface, and spreads, blurring from itself, with the edges of the letters appearing like the microfilm of flies' feet. A nurse brings two small chipped enamel bowls of methylated spirits and ethereal soap, to "rub up" our temples in order that the shock will "take."

I try to find a pair of gray woolen socks for if my feet are cold I know that I shall die. One patient is careful to put on her pants "in case I kick up my legs in front of the doctor." At the last minute, as the feel of nine o'clock surrounds us and we sit in the hard chairs, our heads tipped back, the soaked cotton wool being rubbed on our temples until the skin tears and stings and the dregs of the spirits run down into own ears making sudden blockages of sound, there is a final outbreak of screaming and panicking, attempts by some to grab leftover food from the bed patients, and as a nurse calls "Lavatory, Ladies," and the dormitory door is opened for a brief supervised visit to the doorless lavatories, with guards set in the corridor to prevent escape, there are bursts of fighting and kicking as some attempt to get past, yet realizing almost at once that there is nowhere to run to. The doors to the outside world are locked. You can only be followed and dragged back and if Matron Glass catches you she will speak angrily, "It's for your own good. Pull yourself together. You've been difficult long enough."

The matron herself does not offer to undergo shock treatment in the way that suspected persons to prove their innocence are sometimes willing to take the first slice of the cake that may contain arsenic.

Floral screens are drawn to conceal the end of the dormitory where the treatment beds have been prepared, the sheets rolled back and the pillows placed at an angle, ready to receive the unconscious patient. And now everybody wants to go again to the lavatory, and again, as the panic grows, and the nurse locks the door for the last time, and the lavatory is inaccessible. We yearn to go there, and sit on the cold china bowls and in the simplest way try to relieve ourselves of the mounting distress in our minds, as if a process of the body could change the distress and flush it away as burning drops of water.

And now there is the sound of an early morning catarrhal cough, the springing squeak of rubber-soled shoes on the polished corridor outside, syncopated with the hasty ping-pong steps of cuban-heeled duty shoes, and Dr. Howell and Matron Glass arrive, she unlocking the dormitory door and standing aside while he enters, and both passing in royal procession to join Sister Honey already waiting in the treatment room. At the last minute, because there are not enough nurses, the newly appointed Social Worker who has been asked to help with treatment comes leaping in (we call her Pavlova).

"Nurse, will you send up the first patient."

Many times I have offered to go first because I like to remind myself that by the time I am awake, so brief is the period of unconsciousness, most of the group will still be waiting in a daze of anxiety which sometimes confuses them into thinking that perhaps they have had treatment, perhaps it has been sneaked upon them without their being aware of it.

The people behind the screen begin to moan and cry.

We are taken strictly according to "volts."

We wait while the Ward Two people are "done."

We know the rumors attached to E.S.T.—it is training for Sing Sing when we are at last convicted of murder and sentenced to death and sit strapped in the electric chair with the electrodes touching our skin through slits in our clothing; our hair is singed as we die and the last smell in our nostrils is the smell of ourselves burning. And the fear leads in some patients to more madness. And they say it is a session to get you to talk, that your secrets are filed and kept in the treatment room, and I have had proof of this, for I have passed through the treatment room with a basket of dirty linen, and seen my card. Impulsive and dangerous, it reads. Why? And how? How? What does it all mean?

It is nearly my turn. I walk down to the treatment room door to wait, for so many treatments have to be performed that the doctor becomes impatient at any delay. Production, as it were, is speeded up (like laundry economics—one set of clothes on, one set clean, one in the wash) if there is a patient waiting at the door, one on the treatment table, and another being given a final "rub-up" ready to take her place at the door.

Suddenly the inevitable cry or scream sounds from behind the closed doors which after a few minutes swing open and Molly or Goldie or Mrs. Gregg, convulsed and snorting, is wheeled out. I close my eyes tight as the bed passes me, yet I cannot escape seeing it, or the other beds where people are lying, perhaps heavily asleep, or whimperingly awake, their faces flushed, their eyes bloodshot. I can hear someone moaning and weeping; it is someone who has woken up in the wrong time and place, for I know that the treatment snatches these things from you leaves you alone and blind in a nothingness of being and you try to fumble your way like a newborn animal to the flowing of first comforts; then you wake, small and frightened, and the tears keep falling in a grief that you cannot name.

Beside me is the bed, sheets turned back pillow arranged where I will lie after treatment. They will lift me into it and I shall not know. I look at the bed as if I must establish contact with it. Few people have advance glimpses of their coffin; if they did they might be tempted to charm it into preserving in the satin lining a few trinkets of their identity. In my mind, I slip under the pillow of my treatment bed a docket of time and place so that when and if I ever wake I shall not be wholly confused in a panic of scrabbling through the darkness of not knowing and of being nothing. I go into the room then. How brave I am! Everybody remarks on my bravery! I climb on to the treatment table. I try to breathe deeply and evenly as I have heard it is wise in moments of fear. I try not to mind when the matron whispers to one of the nurses, in a hoarse voice like an assassin, "Have you got the gag?"

And over and over inside myself I am saying a poem

which I learned at school when I was eight. I say the poem, as I wear the gray woolen socks, to ward off Death. They are not relevant lines because very often the law of extremity demands an attention to irrelevancies; the dying man wonders what they will think when they cut his toenails; the man in grief counts the cups in a flower. I see the face of Miss Swap who taught us the poem. I see the mole on the side of her nose, its two mounds like a miniature cottage loaf and the sprout of ginger hair growing out the top. I see myself standing in the classroom reciting and feeling the worn varnished desk top jutting against my body against my bellybutton that has specks of grit in it when I put my finger in; I see from the corner of my left eye my neighbor's pencil case which I coveted because it was a triple decker with a rose design on the lid and a wonderful dent thumb-size for sliding the lid along the groove.

"Moonlit Apples," I say. "By John Drinkwater."

At the top of the house the apples are laid in rows
And the skylight lets the moonlight in and those
Apples are deep-sea apples of green.

I get no further than three lines. The doctor busily attending the knobs and switches of the machine which he respects because it is his ally in the struggle against overwork and the difficulties depressions obsessions manias of a thousand women, has time to smile a harassed Good Morning before he gives the signal to Matron Glass.

"Close your eyes," Matron says.

But I keep them open, observing the secretive signal and engulfed with helplessness while the matron and four nurses and Pavlova press upon my shoulders and my knees and I feel myself dropping as if a trap door had opened into darkness. I imagine as I fall my eyes turning inward to face and confound each other with a separate truth which they prove without my help. Then I rise disembodied from the dark to grasp and attach myself like a homeless parasite to the shape of my identity and its position in space and time. At first I cannot find my way, I cannot find myself where I left myself, someone has removed all trace of me. I am crying.

A cup of sweet tea is being poured down my throat. I grasp the nurse's arm.

"Have I had it? Have I had it?"

"You have had treatment," she answers. "Now go to sleep. You are awake too early."

But I am wide awake and the anxiety begins again to accumulate.

Will I be for treatment tomorrow?

III

 *A*FTER THE DOCTOR performed the last
shock treatment of the morning he used to go with Matron
Glass and Sister Honey for morning tea in Sister's office
where he sat in the best chair brought in from the adjoining
room called the "mess-room" where visitors were sometimes
received. Dr. Howell drank from the special cup which was
tied around the handle with red cotton to distinguish the
staff cups from those of the patients, and thus prevent the in-
terchange of diseases like boredom loneliness authoritarian-
ism. Dr. Howell was young catarrhal plump pale-faced (we
called him *Scone*) short-sighted sympathetic over-worked
with his fresh enthusiasm quickly perishing under con-
centrated stress, like a new plane that is put in a testing
chamber simulating the conditions of millions of miles
of flying and in a few hours suffers the metal fatigue
of years.

The morning tea was followed at eleven o'clock by the
ritual of Rounds when, accompanied by the ubiquitous
Matron Glass and Sister Honey, both acting as go-betweens
interpreters and pickets, Dr. Howell would enter the dayroom where the elderly ladies and those younger but not

27

yet fit for work in the laundry or the sewing room or, higher on the social scale, the Nurses' Home, sat drearily turning over the pages of an old *Illustrated London News* or a *Women's Weekly;* or knitting blanket squares for the lepers; or doing fancywork under the supervision of the newly appointed Occupational Therapist who, it was rumored, much to the dismay of many of the hundred women in Ward Four, was having an affair with Dr. Howell.

"Good morning. How are you today?" the doctor would pause sometimes to inquire, smiling in a friendly manner, but at the same time glancing hastily at his watch and perhaps wondering how in the hour before lunch he could possibly finish his rounds of all the women's wards and get back to his office to deal with correspondence and interviews with demanding puzzled alarmed ashamed relatives.

The patient chosen for conversation with the doctor would become so excited at this rare privilege that she sometimes didn't know what to say or else began a breathless account which was cut short by Matron.

"Now doctor's too busy to listen to that, Marion. You get on with your fancywork."

And in an aside to the doctor the omnipotent Matron would whisper, "She's been rather uncooperative lately. We've put her down for treatment tomorrow."

The doctor would nod absent-mindedly, make a fatuous remark and because of his intelligence immediately realize the fatuity and mentally step back from himself like a salesman who has slighted his own wares. He would point with an increase of eagerness to a tapestry or a ring of lazy-daisy stitch thrust before him by a proud patient. Then, giving a troubled guilty glance around the dayroom, he would retreat for the door while Matron Glass and Sister Honey attended to the mechanics of his exit, unlocking and locking the door and keeping at bay those patients whose need to communicate to a sympathetic listener made them hurry forward in a last attempt to show their tapestry or hurl abuse or greet-and-demand with, Hello Doctor when can I go home?

Sometimes, as if in defiance of Matron Glass and Sister Honey, Dr. Howell chose to isolate himself from them and leave the dayroom by the door which opened on to the spacious tree-filled Ward Four Park; then Matron and Sister would stand looking with accusation at each other and with apprehension as the doctor moved away from them; as spiders might look when a so-carefully-webbed fly with one flick of his wings escapes.

It was the youth of Dr. Howell which appealed to us; the other doctors who did not look after us but who were in charge of the hospital were gray-haired and elderly and hurried in and out of their offices down in front of the building like rats in and out of their hiding places; and they sat, in their work, with the same old chewed solutions littered about them, like nesting material. It was Dr. Howell who tried to spread the interesting news that mental patients were people and therefore might like occasionally to engage in the activities of people. Thus were born "The Evenings" when we played cards—snap, old maid, donkey and euchre; and ludo and snakes and ladders, with prizes awarded and supper afterwards. But where was the extra staff to supervise the activities? Pavlova, the one Social Worker for the entire hospital, valiantly attended a few "social" evenings held for men and women patients in the Ward Four dayroom. She watched people mount ladders and slide down chutes and travel home on the red and blue squares of parcheesi. She too was pleased when the climax of the evening came with the arrival of Dr. Howell in sport coat and soft shoes, with his corn-colored hair slicked down and his undoctorly laugh sounding loud and full. He was like a god; he joined in the games and threw the dice with the aplomb of a god hurling a thunderbolt; he put on the appropriate expression of dismay when he was ordered to slide down a chute, but you could see that he was a charmer even of bile-green cardboard snakes. And of people. He was Pavlova's god too, we knew that; but no amount of leaping about in her soiled white coat with the few bottom buttons undone could help her to steal Dr. Howell from the occupational therapist. Poor Pavlova! And Poor Noeline, who was waiting for Dr. Howell to propose to her although the only words he had even spoken to her were How are you? Do you know where you are? Do you know why you are here?—phrases which ordinarily would be hard to interpret as evidence of affection. But when you are sick you find in yourself a new field of perception where you make a harvest of interpretations which then provides you with your daily bread, your only food. So that when Dr. Howell finally married the occupational therapist, Noeline was taken to the disturbed ward. She could not understand why the doctor did not need her more than anyone else in the world, why he had betrayed her to marry someone whose only virtue seemed to be the ability to show patients who were not always interested, how to weave scarves and make shadow stitch on muslin.

IV

*I*T IS SAID that when a prisoner is condemned to die all clocks in the neighborhood of the death cell are stopped; as if the removal of the clock will cut off the flow of time and maroon the prisoner on a coast of time-lessness where the moments, like breakers, rise and surge near but never touch the shore.

But no death of an oceanographer ever stopped the sea flowing; and a condition of sea is its meeting with the land. And in the death cell time flows in as if all the cuckoo clocks grandfather clocks alarm clocks were striking simultaneously in the ears of the prisoner.

Again and again when I think of Cliffhaven I play the time game, as if I have been condemned to die and the signals have been removed yet I hear them striking in my ears, warning me that nine o'clock, the time of treatment, is approaching and that I must find myself a pair of woolen socks in order that I shall not die. Or it is eleven o'clock and treatment is over and it is the early hours or years of my dream when I was not yet sitting in rainbow puddles in Ward Two Yard or tramping the shorn park inside the tall picket fence with its rusty nails sprouting from the top, their points to the sky.

Eleven o'clock. I remember eleven o'clock, the pleasant agony of trying to decide when plump pale-faced Mrs. Pilling ready with the laundry basket with the cheese-smelling tablecloth inside would ask me, "Will you come for the bread with me?"

And at the same time anxious Mrs. Everett who was detained in hospital, as they say, "at the sovereign's pleasure" would appear with an empty milk jug and ask "Will you come with me to collect the cream for the specials?"

The prospect of two journeys at the same time beyond the locked doors was so full of delight that I dallied to savor the pleasure and to hold a debate with myself on the merits of bakery and separator room. Bread or cream? The bakery with Andy shoveling the trays of loaves like yeasted molars into the yawning oven, slicing our ward bread and trying to sing above the slicer a duet for baker and bread machine with incidental crusts, or perhaps inviting me into the back room to give me a pastry left over from the Superintendent's party, or an advance chunk of the currant-filled Sunday Borstal cake.

Or the walk up the hill to the farm, past the deserted dung-smelling cowsheds into the separator room where Ted had arranged the cream cans in order of importance the way we used as children to arrange cups—first in the class, second in the class, and so on, when we played school with them.

First, the Superintendent's can, well polished with no dents and no ridge of old cream inside the shoulders. Next, the can for the doctors, also cleaned. Then for the Chief Clerk the farm manager and his family the engineer matrons and head attendant the attendants and nurses.

Finally, the special patients who were too frail or suffered from tuberculosis and whose names appeared on a list pinned to the dining room wall. From a ward of one hundred women only ten or fifteen could be "special" enough to have cream. I remember my amazement and gratitude when for some weeks my name appeared on the list of "specials" and I sat smugly at dinner while the nurse poured cream on my tapioca or rice or farina or bread pudding (Mondays) or (Thursdays in season) baked apple.

You know that I have been pretending; you know that it is eleven o'clock and I am not allowed to go for the bread or up the hill past the poplar trees and the broom bushes and the wattle to fetch the cream; that I am hiding in the linen cupboard, sitting on an apple box of firewood and crying and afraid to be seen crying in case I am written up for E.S.T. The linen cupboard is my favorite hiding place. It is scrubbed every morning by the T.B. nurse and the floor looks like the deck of a ship. From here I listen to Margaret who has T.B. and whose hoarse whisper tells continually of the First World War. She pleads with any-one who passes in the corridor to help her to evict the enemy from her room. She has lived for many years in this room, seeing the sun only for a few hours on a summer afternoon when shafts of light maneuver their way through the rusted wire netting of the window to shine and set the motes dancing on the wall. Sometimes on an afternoon walk with the nurse you can see Margaret standing in the sunlit corner of her room; the sun seems to shine through her as if the texture of her bones were gossamer. Her face is without color, even without the two familiar fever spots on her cheeks, and her body is like a skeleton. Looking at her you think, She is dying. Yet she goes on living, year after year, while other consumptives more robust on appearance—Effie, Jane, die and their bodies are hastily and antiseptically dispatched to the mortuary which is at the back of the laundry, facing the greenhouse, surrounded by rows of flowers and vegetables, the hardy plants outside and, inside, the sensitive begonias in pots used for surrounding the piano when the blind man from the city comes to play.

The mortuary is faceless.

If it were built in proportion, to really house the dead, its size would swallow the greenhouse and the laundry and the boiler house and the Big Kitchen, perhaps the entire hospital. But it is small, unobtrusive, and begs that patients conform to the rule of loneliness by dying one at a time.

In spite of the scrubbed appearance of the linen cupboard the smell pervading it is of floor polish boot polish (from the little-used caked tins of black and brown kept inside the large dented biscuit tin which bears on its lid the earnest profile of George the Sixth); wet-stained chipped wood whose smell leaves a parched blocked taste in the mouth; clinging wet linen; and the muffled ironed smell of fresh linen on the shelves labeled Drawers Chemises Nightgowns Sheets Counterpanes (with their scrolled patriotic design *Ake Ake*, Onward Onward). Here are kept the T.B. masks and dishes and the cardboard sputum boxes as they are procured, unfolded, from the stores. The T.B.'s, as part of their realistic occupational therapy, spend some of their time folding the boxes tucking in the flaps setting them upright with the ounces clearly marked on the side;

like a kindergarten class engaged in constructing do-it-your-self coffins. Here are the cut-down kerosene tins where the used T.B. dishes are put to be boiled, for there is yet no sterilizer for them, on the open fire in the dining room.

This process is supervised by Mrs. Everett and Mrs. Pilling who share control of kitchen affairs and are responsible for the fire. It is Mrs. Pilling (the most trusted patient in the ward) who also arranges the making of toast over the open fire in the morning, the collecting of bread and cream, the carrying out to the side door of the full pig-tin ready for the golden-haired pig-boy to pick up on his way to the farm driving the leisurely old cart horse. When the tin has been loaded on the back he rummages through the food, bypassing the cold skilly bog of leftover porridge and reaching for the more appetizing dainties of discarded toast and sodden pieces of currant bun, all of which he stuffs hungrily in his mouth and, chewing contentedly, climbs again to the front of the cart and with a tug of the reins and a "Gee-up" sets the morose but patient horse on his way. Mrs. Pilling in her undemonstrative silent manner has an understanding with the pig-boy and though she recoils from his habits she has a stolid tolerance and respect for other people's peculiarities and is inclined to act out of character herself in order to preserve someone else's individuality.

She sometimes leaves a slice of staff cake on the pig-tin. It seems that she has no husband no children no relatives. She never has visitors. She never speaks of her personal concerns; one is seldom aware that she has any. She has lived for many years in the hospital and has a small room at the end of the T.B. corridor; one is surprised on passing it to notice that it has a cosy appearance as far as that is possible in a room in a mental hospital. She is allowed to keep her overcoat. It hangs behind the door. There is a feminine smell of powder and clothes. At one time someone must have given her a potted plant; it now stands on a chair in one corner, and an old calendar of five years ago, presumably kept for its old-fashioned English country scene, hangs over the hole in the center of the door so that the nurses may not peep in at her in the night. She is allowed that privacy.

Her sobriety, her apparent acceptance of a way of life that will continue until she dies—these frighten me. She seems like someone who could set up camp in a graveyard and continue to boil the billy, eat and sleep soundly and perhaps spend the day polishing the tombstones or weeding the graves. One watches her for a ripple of herself as one watches an eternally calm lake for evidence of the rumored creature inhabiting perhaps "deeper than ever plummet sounded." One needs a machine like a bathysphere to find Mrs. Pilling. A bathysphere of fear? Of love?

In the beginning and the end her life is bread cream building the dining room fire; making sure with Mrs. Everett, who also has a passion for polishing, that the copper tea-urn is given its daily shine; setting out the Private Cupboard food. Fruit sweets cakes biscuits brought by visitors and not eaten during the Saturday and Sunday visiting hours are taken from the patients and locked in the Private Cupboard and at teatime, depending on how much food has been stored for you, you find beside your place at the table a dish with your name on it containing perhaps two or three wrapped chocolates an orange an

36

apple. Sometimes, because I seldom have visitors, I contrive to help Mrs. Pilling and the nurse and wait greedily for the expected moment when the nurse arranging on a plate a glittering still life of chocolates says suddenly, "Here, have one."

I protest, "Oh no. They do not belong to me."

The nurse answers according to plan, "No, this patient has bags and bags of food; it's going to waste."

Guiltily I seize the chocolate unwrap it slowly smoothe the wrinkles from the silver paper take a small bite testing for hardness then, like a thief, like the cunning scrounger that I am, I eat it. In the same way after visitors leave and the patients depressed and agitated talking about husband home children are wandering around clutching their only visible and palpable remnants of visiting hour, their small collection of biscuits sweets fruit, then I, with nothing in my hand and trying calmly to answer the question "Who came to see you?" will "happen" to appear in the most crowded corner of the dayroom where I know I will be offered an orange or a peppermint or a biscuit.

"You should keep them for yourself," I protest, greedily holding out my hand.

There is no past present or future. Using tenses to divide time is like making chalk marks on water. I do not know if my experiences at Cliffhaven happened years ago, are happening now, or lie in wait for me in what is called the future.

I know that the linen room was very often my sanctuary. I looked through its little dusty window upon the lower park and the lawns and trees and the distant blue strip of sea like sticky paper pasted edge to edge with the sky. I wept and wondered and dreamed the abiding dream of most mental patients—The World, Outside, Freedom; and foretasted too vividly the occasions I most feared—electric shock treatment, being shut in a single room at night, being sent to Ward Two, the disturbed ward. I dreamed of the world because it seemed the accepted thing to do, because I could not bear to face the thought that not all prisoners dream of freedom; the prospect of the world terrified me: a morass of despair violence death with a thin layer of glass spread upon the surface where Love, a tiny crab with pincers and rainbow shell, walked delicately ever sideways but getting nowhere, while the sun—like one of those woolly balls we made at occupational therapy by winding orange wool on a circle of cardboard—rose higher in the sky its tassels dropping with flame threatening every moment to melt the precarious highway of glass. And the people: giant patchworks of color with limbs missing and parts of their mind snipped off to fit them into the outline of the free pattern.

I could not find my way from the dream; I had no means to escape from it; I was like a surgeon who at the moment of a delicate operation finds that his tray of instruments has been stolen, or, worse, twisted into unfamilar shapes so that only he can realize their unfamiliarity while the team around the table, suspecting nothing, wait for him to make the first incision. How can he explain to them what they cannot understand because it is visible only to him? Dutifully I thought of The World, because I was beyond it—who else will dream of it with longing? And at times I murmured the token phrase to the doctor, "When can I go home?" knowing that home was the place where I least desired to be. There they would watch me for signs of abnormality, like ferrets around a rabbit burrow waiting for the rabbit to appear.

I feared the prospect of a single room. Although all the small rooms were "single" rooms the use of the phrase *single room* served to make a threat more terrifying. During my stay in Ward Four I slept first in the Observation Dormitory and later in the dormitory "down the other end" where the beds had floral bedspreads and where, because of the lack of space, there was an overflow of beds into the corridor. I liked the observation dormitory at night with the night nurse sitting in the armchair brought in from the mess-room, knitting an endless number of cardigans and poring over pull-out pattern supplements in the women's magazines, and snatching a quick nap with her feet up on the fireguard and the fire pleasantly warming her bottom. I liked the ritual of going to bed, with the faithful Mrs. Pilling sending in a tray of hot milk drinks, and one of the patients marching in balancing like a waitress a high pile of dun-colored chambers. I liked the beds side by side and the reassurance of other people's soft breathing mingled with the irritation of their snoring and their secret conversations and the tinkle-tinkle and warm smell like a cow byre when they used their chambers in the night. I dreaded that one day Matron Glass hearing that I had been "difficult" or "uncooperative" would address me sharply, "Right. Single room for you, my lady."

Hearing other people threatened so often made me more afraid, and seeing that a patient, in the act of being taken to a single room, always struggled and screamed, made me morbidly curious about what the room contained that, over-night, it could change people who screamed and disobeyed into people who sat, withdrawn, and obeyed listlessly when ordered Dayroom, Dining room, Bed. Yet not all people changed; and those who did not respond to the four-square shuttered influence of the room, who could not be taught what Matron Glass or Sister Honey decreed to be "a lesson," were removed to Ward Two.

And Ward Two was my fear. They sent you there if you were "uncooperative" or if persistent doses of E.S.T. did not produce in you an improvement which was judged largely by your submission and prompt obedience to orders —Dayroom Ladies, Rise Ladies, Bed Ladies.

You learned with earnest dedication to "fit in"; you learned not to cry in company but to smile and pronounce yourself pleased, and to ask from time to time if you could go home, as proof that you were getting better and therefore in no need of being smuggled in the night to Ward Two. You learned the chores, to make your bed with the government motto facing the correct way and the corners of the counterpane neatly angled; to "rub up" the dormitory and the corridor, working the heavy bumper on the piece of torn blanket smeared with skittery yellow polish that distributed its energetic soaking smell from the first day it was fetched with the weekly stores in the basket beside the tins of jam jars of vinegar and the huge blocks of cheese and butter which Mrs. Pilling and Mrs. Everett quarried with a knife specially unlocked from the knife box. You learned the routine, that it "was so," that bath night was Wednesday, but that those who could be trusted to wash further than their wrists were allowed to bathe any night in the large bathroom where the roof soared like in a railway station and three deep tubs lay side by side each with its locked box containing the taps. In small print so that one might mistake it for a railway timetable the list of bathing rules was pasted on the wall. It was an old list, issued at the beginning of the century, and contained fourteen rules which stated, for example, that no patient might take a bath unless an attendant were present, that six inches only of water should be run into the bath, the cold water first, that no brush of any kind should be employed in bathing a patient. . . . So we bathed, one in each bath, without screens, gazing curiously at one another's bodies, at the pendulous bellies and tired breasts, the faded wisps of body hair, the unwieldy and the supple shapes that form to women the nagging and perpetual "withness" of their flesh.

V

"SETTLING IN?" the doctor would inquire from time to time, as a passing breeze from another country might address an animal which it happened to catch sight of preparing for hibernation. The act of "settling in" was surrounded with approval: "the sooner you 'settle' the sooner you'll be allowed home" was the ruling logic; and "if you can't adapt yourself to living in a mental hospital how do you expect to be able to live 'out in the world'?" How indeed?

In the early days I looked with pity and curiosity and wonder upon the few patients in the observation ward who would be there "forever"—Mrs. Pilling, Mrs. Everett who, as an inexperienced overwrought young mother, had murdered her little girl; Miss Dennis, slight, sharp tongued, with neatly rolled gray hair, whose days were devoted to "doing out" the Charge Room at the Nurses' Home, polishing the silver and the water glasses and the fruit dishes of the illustrious white-veiled sisters; and the few other permanent patients who comprised those who knew the rules and could explain them—how when you were well enough you were given limited parole and when you were very well and trusted (as most of these patients were) you were given full parole and allowed to wander where you wished in the hospital grounds; how on leaving the hospital you were not immediately discharged but placed on probation, as if you had committed a criminal offense, so that you might be away from the hospital and still be legally insane, unable to vote, to sign papers or travel abroad. In "those days" there was no voluntary admission; we were all "insane under the Mental Defectives' Act, 1928."

These long-term patients who were more like employees of the hospital could discuss the hierarchy of the staff, the private life of the Matron who lived in a flat in the front of the building. Minnie, from Ward One, was the matron's personal maid and was allowed a key and used to come through the ward during the day with the papers and the latest gossip from 'down the front' which she passed on to Mrs. Everett and Mrs. Pilling and, particularly, Miss Dennis who liked to reinforce her superiority of manner with the superiority of being well-informed.

We learned of the life of the doctors from Carrie, from Ward One, who worked at the doctors' flat, and from Molly, who worked over the road for another doctor and his family. "His wife nags," she said—triumphantly, for it seemed to strengthen his bonds with patients who, it seemed, were ready to "understand" him. So we, the newcomers, learned of important events like Christmas ("they put all the tables together for Christmas dinner; we have pork and applesauce; everybody gets a present.") Churchgoing, Dances (as part of the "new" attitude to mental patients dances were now being held), the hospital sports, the opening of the bowling green, the cricket match between the hospital and the village, the visit of the One-Lolly Man from the Patients and Prisoners Aid Society.

The other permanent patients lived in Ward Two. Except at E.S.T. we saw little of these people. We heard them as background noises from their special park and yard and at night when their sleeping quarters, known as the Brick Building, became like a hive with the bees wailing and screaming behind the rusted wire-netting windows, as if their day's honey had been lost or never gathered. Sometimes we saw them in the evening being rushed into the Brick Building and seeming to execute a wild dance before they entered, as if to signal the direction of the flowerless fields where for one more day in the numerous years of their search they had wasted their time and yearning. And occasionally we glimpsed these same people in their dark blue striped smocks their skin sun stained and wrinkled being driven, flanked by nurses, from the dayroom of their ward to the park where they would spend the rest of the day. And then they looked, sad to say, like people; we could not deny their relationship to us; but they moved their heads, bowed, their bodies half crouching, as if they faced a driving blizzard, as if they pushed on to a kind of One Ton Camp of the soul, with no hope of getting there.

Or sometimes when Church was held by the chaplain in the hospital hall and we attended out of boredom or out of a desire like Lear and Cordelia in prison to "pray and sing," a restless group from Ward Two would be led in and persuaded to sit on the long wooden seats. They sang with a gusto which seemed to disturb the minister standing soberly and self-consciously before his lectern, his Bible lying open at the lesson of comfort which he read rather guiltily and sentimentally. The Ward Two people in their curious assortment of Ward hats behaved like excited children bobbing up and down and interrupting the sermon with well-placed remarks. They smiled placidly when prayers were offered "for those sick in mind." They sang fervently

> Shall we gather at the river
> The beautiful beautiful river
> Shall we gather at the river
> That flows by the throne of God.

and

> Summer suns are glowing
> Over land and sea
> Happy light is flowing
> Bountiful and free.

The men sat on one side of the hall, the women on the other. Beneath the surface activities of church, notes were passed escapes plotted endearments exchanged. The men's voices, prolonged and powerful if sometimes out of tune, often showed unwillingness to abandon a satisfying last note, keeping the sympathetic organist, a woman from Ward One who was the image of George the Third, playing on with soporific everlastingness until the chaplain, whose appreciation of eternity was dependent on its elusiveness and who felt reluctant to accept its materialization as the A-Men of *Shall We Gather at the River* or *Jesus Shall Reign Where'er the Sun*, would determinedly interrupt, raising his voice to pronounce the blessing, "And now may the Grace of the Lord Jesus Christ abide with us each one now and forever more."

The Ward Two people liked to stay behind to shake hands with the chaplain and talk to him of domestic affairs, but we, the Ward Four people, feeling alarmed at their friendliness as if perhaps it were a symptom of the infection of permanence that might too easily spread to us, hurried from the hall and across our daisy-covered park to our own ward. Not one of the strenuously applied platitudes could fit the people of Ward Two.

"They're happy in their own way."

"They're so far gone they don't really suffer."

"They're used to it, they don't realize any more."

"Nothing makes any difference to them."

They haunted me, not the few articulate ones who had been to church, but those I glimpsed sometimes through the fence into the park or the yard. Who were they? Why were they in hospital? Why were they so changed from people that you see walking and talking in the streets of the World? And what was the meaning of the gifts or rejects which they threw over the park and yard fence—pieces of cloth, crusts, feces, shoes—in a barrage of love and hate for what lay beyond?

VI

*S*UNDAY DINNER, roast mutton, was carved, like the other dinners of the week, by Matron Glass who went from ward to ward for the purpose, picking on her way a few tidbits to "test" the cooking. The meat was forked on to the plates by Sister Honey standing behind the long serving table; the vegetables were dolloped on by the next in command, while Mrs. Everett, flushed and anxious in case, having been too generous with the first few helpings, she had to "go canny" with the remainder, poured on the weed-green mint sauce. Now the serving was ready and we moved from the queue to take our place at the table and await the final serving and the saying of grace by Sister Honey, For what you are about to receive the Lord make you truly thankful. Only then could we set about eating the now lukewarm roast and greens and potatoes lying in their stiff overcoats of fat. There was no obligation to eat, although we were frequently warned that "others are worse off on the other side of the world," with the convenient propensity that people show for making hunger grief any discomfort antipodean.

Sometimes with unexpected charity which earned our

gratitude and made us realize that she was "human after all," Sister Honey let us eat first, and said grace after the meal when the knives had been collected counted and locked in their box and we were sitting waiting for the mail and announcements which were usually warnings of misdoings, and began "Now in future I don't want . . ." or "Some of the patients have been reported as . . ." to which we listened with fearful attention.

Yet Sister Honey did not rule entirely by fear; she had spurts of gaiety which found their expression in what she called "get-togethers" around the ward piano of an evening, when she would take off her red cardigan, in a liberal gesture, and hang it on the back of a chair, and sit down at the piano and play for us the songs usually of another generation, demanding in her sharp voice, "Come on sing up everyone."

> *When there's a rainbow on the river*
> *You get the feeling*
> *Romance is stealing*
> *Right out of the blue into your heart.*

and *When Irish Eyes Are Smiling* and *Road to the Isles*, ending with a hymn,

> *There is a green hill far away*
> *Without a city wall*
> *Where the dear Lord was crucified*
> *Who died to save us all.*

At this point Sister's expression would become severe and she would turn to look meaningfully at us as if to say Remember you've got something to be grateful for, so pull yourselves together, snap out of it, everything is being done for your own good, there are others far worse off than you, my ladies.

Then with a slightly bitter smile around her thin unpainted lips she would play a dance tune and tell us to get up and dance with one another to finish the evening. When she left the dayroom after this display of straight-backed comradeship people remarked, "She's a sport anyway."

And the next morning she would look at us grimly and coldly as she made the announcement, "No breakfast for you. You're for treatment."

Sunday was a pleasant day compared with the rest of the week. No shock treatment, church in the morning, in the afternoon a walk in the grounds perhaps up past the poplars away up the hill past the wooden building where some of the men lived, the old doddering ones who could only sit out in the sun and the younger mongols and imbeciles who gave a simple help around the farm and in the garden. A rope clothesline sagging with their striped ward clothes was stretched between two poles at the back door. Sometimes we saw a face peering at us from the curtainless windows; or a little group sitting in the sun staring, their lips moving in the way old people have, as if in their life they have never been able to say what they needed to say or have never had anyone to say it to, and now when they are old they babble on and on not minding the words, only to get it said in time. While you are alive and persist in the sovereign act of living you are surrounded by invisible courtiers of being which keep

49

your self spruce and well fed, as the bees attend their queen; but when you are near death these courtiers neglect you or even join forces to kill you and you acquire the inner, unkempt look of the dying. The unkemptness of these old men showed from within, beyond the shabby appearance of their braces hitching their pants anyhow, their unbuttoned flies, their flannel shirts bunched out, hanging loose.

When we passed their dining room and looked in at the bare wooden tables already laid for tea with the thick cup, plate and spoon at each place, I was depressed by the dreariness of a day where tea is prepared for immediately after dinner. After tea, no doubt, the old men were put to bed at once, in the daylight. I wanted to go in the dining room and put a white cloth and flowers on the long tables. The authorities in some of the hospital wards of the world had learned—it had been reported in the newspapers, with headlines—that flowers "helped." Could they have helped in this men's ward? Perhaps not. It seemed to be a place where there was no one home. I was reminded of the times when my father used to come home from work and my mother was perhaps in the garden or the lavatory or talking to one of the neighbors over the fence, and a look of panic would cross my father's face as he walked into the empty kitchen.

"Where's Mum?" he would say.

And I was reminded of a poem we used to say at school, a mysterious poem beginning, " 'Is there anyone there?' said the traveler, knocking on the moonlit door." A traveler could knock for years at the door of that dismal ward; he could even shout, like the traveler in the poem, "Tell them

I came!" and he could get no answer. The old men were dead though their mouths moved and they snaffled their tea and Borstal cake; though they sat in the gentle sun with their long sharp afternoon shadows, their only companions, lying motionless and dumb beside them.

On our walk we also visited the calf paddock where the knock-kneed Friesians thrust their heads through the fence to us, sucking with their raspy tongues on our extended hands. Or we walked, holding our noses, through the pigsties watching the piglets like pink sausages side by side feeding from their supine frowsy mothers; or the half-grown pigs nuzzling the ward leftovers and snorting in the trough swilled with skim milk. Did the pigs realize that on our ward dining room wall they had a notice all to themselves?

"Please do not put fish bones in the pig-tin. Valuable pigs have been lost through this practice."

Up near the sties we would stand on the hill and look out and down at the sea, at the smoke on the horizon of a ship carrying wheat or coal to one of the East Coast ports; nearer, below us were the gray slated roofs of the hospital's main building with its small barred windows built to resist the arrows of light, and the tower with its bell like an ancient prison bell which still tolled heavily morning and evening.

Or we walked down towards the front garden past the sacred enclosure marked *Trespassing forbidden*, where the Superintendent lived. We would dawdle on, our pace being set by the slowest walker, until we halted at the cattle stop by the front gate beyond which lay the World—the tiny grassy village of Cliffhaven with its school and church and two general stores, and, down the road past the doctor's house, its railway station and the red wooden enclosure, like a school playroom that was the waiting room, where the seagulls flew inside leaving black and gray mottled splashes on the floor, where abandoned luggage was piled in the corner as if it had lain there for many years; where the broken-hinged door led to the lavatory with the rusty drip marks down its bowl and in the wash basin, the pool of water on the floor, and the scrap of toilet paper half covering the darkened mound of somebody's business not flushed away.

We stood at the gate, considering the marvel of the World where people, such is the deception of memory, did as they pleased, owned furniture, dressing tables with doilies on them and wardrobes with mirrors; and doors they could open and shut and open as many times as they chose; and no name tapes sewn inside the neck of their clothes; and handbags to carry, with nail files and make-up; and no one to watch while they were eating and to collect and count the knives afterwards and say in a frightening voice, "Rise, Ladies."

We retraced our steps then up the gravel path to Ward Four. The door would be unlocked for us and we would be led down the corridor past the T.B. rooms and the old ladies' rooms and Mrs. Pilling's room, to the coat-cupboard to remove our coats and scarves and, except for the guileful few (sometimes including myself) who could persuade the nurse that they "always" helped to set the tables for tea or "never missed" attending to the eggs for the observation dormitory while they boiled on the dining room fire or "usually" wheeled the tea trolley along to the dormitory, we were locked in the dayroom until teatime. There the others too old or too ill who had not been out walking looked up dully as we entered with our cheeks pink, excited with what we had seen—the pigs the calves the doctor's washing on the line the magnolia tree (the pride of the hospital) in bloom. And we had been to the gate, to the cattle stop at the gate!

The people stared; they were not impressed. They continued staring, some moaning softly, others going through the worn routine of rattling at the dayroom door, of calling for help; others gazing from the wide windows at the trees, the copper beech tree shining in the afternoon sun and the fir trees and the blackbirds in their low flight across the grass.

What did it matter that we had been to the gate, to the cattle stop, to the gate? The people in the dayroom seemed to look at us accusingly as if we had wasted our time by wandering in the grounds. *They* had no need to go for walks; they knew without seeing it the magnolia in bloom. We sat down, subdued, and waited for teatime. Tomorrow was Monday. Keep on your nightgown and dressing gown your nightgown and dressing gown and nightgown nightgown . . .

VII

*A*FTER THREE YEARS of living in Ward
Four and going dutifully for treatment on nearly every
morning when it was required of me, and earning Mrs.
Pilling's respect by my enthusiastic polishing of the corridor and Mrs. Everett's good will by my (sometimes
feigned) willingness to peel apples and polish the silver
on a Friday, and the increasing disapproval of Matron
Glass and Sister Honey by my tendency to panic at mealtimes, I was pronounced well enough to go home. Once
people knew you were going home they looked upon you
with envy and seemed compelled to point you out amongst
themselves and to their visitors, saying, "There's Mona, or
Dolly, or Nancy. She's going home."

"Really?" the visitors would remark, like tourists in a
foreign land when a building they regard as commonplace
is pointed out to them as a marvel. It was as well not to
talk about it if you were going home, not even to say
you were going; you felt the guilt of it and the pleasure;
you felt like a child at an orphanage who has been accepted
for adoption and must face, when your new parents call for
you, the longing gaze of the deprived people around you.

My mother was to call for me. Like the rest of the rest of the family she had been shocked and frightened at the thought that one of her daughters had "landed up" in Cliff-haven. The family notion of people in Cliffhaven, in any mental hospital, was gathered from jokes about loonies—about visiting dignitaries on tours of inspection being asked their name by one of the loonies and when they answer Lord or Sir, meeting with the reply, "You'll soon get over that. I thought I was the King of England when I came here."

My family had not visited me often. They seemed to me strange and remote, and sometimes when I glanced quickly at my mother and father I surprised their bodies falling apart and crumbling, and the cells of their skin like grains of wheat being crushed to a fine powder; sometimes they played tricks on me and vanished and changed to birds beating powerful wings and setting up a storm in the air.

My mother wore new clothes which I did not trust. For years, ever since she had been married, her main article of clothing had been what she called "a nice navy-blue costume." But lately she had sent her outsize measurements to a mail-order firm in the north and had had delivered to her a brown costume with fine brown stripes. She had never worn brown before, not a brown costume, and seemed ill at ease, as if harboring something dishonest, when she came to visit me in her new clothes. Boot-polish brown, with a secret shine and easily stained with grass when we sat down to have our picnic under the copper beech tree.

So my mother came to take me home. She talked in a high excited voice to the doctor assuring him indignantly that of course I have never heard voices or seen things and that there was nothing the matter with me. My mother was suspicious of the doctor; in some way she regarded my illness as a reflection on herself, as something to be ashamed of, to be hushed up, to be denied if necessary. She was deeply indignant but complied with the doctor's suggestion that I should not live at home, that I should go up north and live for a time with my sister who had expressed a willingness to "have me."

I said good-bye to Mrs. Everett and Mrs. Pilling and the baker and the pig-boy and the nurses, the timid new ones filling the coal buckets, cleaning the fireplaces and trying to carry out trays of hot ashes through the draught from the side door, working so hard in their twelve hours a day, looking so flushed and disheveled and tired, with stains of soot on the front of their new pink uniform and red marks around their heels where the stiff duty shoes were rubbing. But they were learning. They were learning to give orders that would be obeyed promptly, and to push into line the wandering herd.

Good-bye, I said, promising to write, and knowing that after the first few letters there would be nothing to say except the kind of phrases which people use like mothballs to try and preserve a period of time: "Does Dr. Howell still come to the Evenings on Mondays? I suppose Pavlova is still the same as ever? Do you still have mince and wallboard pastry on Tuesdays?"

There remained an interview with the Superintendent

who had never spoken to me but whom I had sometimes seen making his Friday rounds, driving from ward to ward along the narrow tree-lined roads in his powerful amply buttocked maroon car with his red setter Molly gazing from the window. Dr. Portman was a plump short dark Englishman with an indulged mustache, and brown eyes glittering beneath creepered brows. He was a man of decisive attitudes and gestures with quick sympathies and a sense of the sublime which exceeded his mental strutting, as if a rooster with purpose and success had taken to wearing buskins. Dr. Portman was nicknamed the "Mad Major."

I knocked and entered his room and stood timidly on the red carpet. On his desk stood a framed motto, in Italian, which read Precious is the passing moment.

"Come and sit down," he said kindly.

I sat down.

He leaned forward. "Have you ever been raped?" he asked. I told him no. He got up from his desk then and came and shook hands with me and wished me well, and I left the hospital.

I was on probation.

VIII

*M*Y MOTHER AND *I* waited on the railway station for the Limited to arrive. I remembered how often, when I had been traveling past Cliffhaven and the train stopped to unload and collect mail and water the engine, I had looked out to see the "loonies" standing on the platform. Now, as the train halted, I watched the faces of the people staring from the carriages and I wondered if I had any distinguishing marks of madness about me, and I wondered if the people understood or wanted to understand what lay beyond the station, up the road over the cattle stop and up the winding path and behind the locked doors of the gray stone building.

I thought as I climbed into the carriage, "Now Mrs. Pilling is putting the bread on the table for tea and Mrs. Everett is boiling the eggs over the dining room fire. Mrs. Ritchie in the dayroom is telling an interested but skeptical audience of the operation in which part of her body "just came away like that. It was a mistake in the operation. Part of my body, a secret part that I cannot name, just came away like that." Gesturing and with her cheeks flushed she emphasizes the deplorable mistake which has made her different from everyone else in the world, and condemns the doctors for their refusal to admit to theft of part of her body. And Susan is standing still and silent in the corner; her limbs are blue and cold. She has taken off her cardigan and shoes and will not be persuaded to put them on again.

And the confused elderly ladies are wandering up and down in their crumpled dresses, with concertina ripples in their lisle stockings, because when they were dressed in the early morning perhaps their garters were missing from their "bundle." They are rattling on the locked door, trying to get out, to "see to" things or make sure of something which has intruded from their past and demands their immediate attention; they need to talk to people who are not there, to minister to the long dead—to make cups of tea for tired husbands who are beyond the dayroom and the grave. Voices convey to them urgent messages; they are beside themselves with anxiety; no one will listen to them or understand.

The very new nurses in their first few days of scrubbing, making beds and filling coal buckets, as if the purpose of their work were to establish relationship with the domestic property of the ward, to heal bucket and blanket and corridor, find it somehow soothing to stand in the dayroom and comb the hair of the old ladies with the coarse-toothed ward comb. It is thinning white hair trailing in wisps over the transparent blue-veined skull. Later, the same nurses will become impatient with their charges; but at first they are full of sympathy; the old ladies are obviously suffering; and their strayed appearance is emphasized by their clothes, the overlong cardigans wrapped over their shrunken bodies, and the seemingly shapeless dresses that husbands or daughters have brought them on visiting day with the words, "I hope it fits but somehow I couldn't think of your right size," perhaps inwardly realizing that for the old ladies there is no "right size," that the deception of their inner world has reached their body and in some way removed it from ordinary forms of measurement.

These old people sit at the special table, have cream on their pudding, and are hurried early to their rooms, undressed, put to bed and locked in. Immediately the nurse is gone they get out of bed and potter around the room making sure looking for things seeing to things. They continue thus, restlessly, most of the night, and in the morning after only fitful sleep, sometimes with their beds wet and dirty, they begin again to try to solve the daily puzzle of being where they are, of not being allowed to go outside, of losing their garters and their handkerchiefs and of being involved in the complexities of going from one place to another, of going to the lavatory and remembering to wipe themselves, of being led from dayroom to meal table and back again. After some weeks, if they do not improve, they will be sent in the big black government car to "Kaikohe" by the sea where the old people go, or will be transferred to Ward One which is also the children's ward with an inner courtyard where yellow grass grows through the cracks in the asphalt and where pale slobbering children play, consoled by their few wooden toys in the daytime and at night sleeping in cots in small damp rooms with concrete floors.

In this ward the old women will eventually be put to bed for the last time; they will lie in the dreary sunless rooms that stink of urine; they will be washed and "turned" daily, and the film, the final deception, will grow over their eyes.

And one morning, if you walk along the corridor through Ward One, you will see in the small room where one of the old women has been sleeping, the floor newly scrubbed smelling of disinfectant, the bed stripped, the mattress turned back to air; the vacancy created in the night by death.

The train drew slowly out of Cliffhaven, gathering speed as it passed the banks untidy with wild sweet peas and gorse and the back gardens with their slapping soapsud-reeking lines of washing and their henhouses, where fat snow-white hens, their behinds in the air, pecked and scratched at the stony soil. I gave up trying to discern the hospital towers through the gaps in the receding hills, and settled into the slothful smoke-tasting attitude of a railway traveler, gazing dreamily at the dead contorted trees and the obsessedly nibbling sheep and the cows, tails aswish, clustering already for milking. Cliffhaven slipped from my mind as easily as the sun was slipping down the sky into the gap between cloud and horizon.

When the train stopped in a wilderness of grass and gum trees and was switched to a siding to give clear passage to the southbound express, and stayed there waiting and waiting, until it seemed that it had been abandoned and would be overtaken by the rust and weeds and silence that threaten all men and machines in rest and motion, I was reminded once more of Cliffhaven and the people there. Did their life in a siding give right-of-way to more urgent traffic? And what was its destination?

But the train moved, and I slept, and did not care. Cliffhaven was far far away, and I would never be sick again. Would I?

PART TWO

Treecroft

*S*O I WENT up north to a land of palm trees and mangroves like malignant growths in the mud-filled throats of the bays, and orange trees with their leaves accepting darkly and seriously, in their own house as it were, the unwarranted globular outbursts of winter flame; and the sky faultless and remote. This was "up north." I stayed for a few weeks with my sister. Have you ever been a spinster living in a small house with your sister and her husband and their new first child? Watching them rub noses and pinch and tickle and in the night, when you lie on the coffin-narrow camp cot that would not hold two people anyway, listening to them because you cannot help it?

I did not know my own identity. I was burgled of body and hung in the sky like a woman of straw. The day seemed palpable about me yet receded when I moved to touch it, for fear that I might contaminate it. I nagged at the sky. It grew protective porcelain filling of cloud. I was not a mosquito nor a cricket nor a bamboo tree, therefore I found myself, when it was full summer, lying in a gaily quilted bed in a spotless room called an observation dormitory in Ward Seven of Treecroft Mental Hospital, up north. The room overlooked a garden of blown roses and orange-centered arum lilies that grow wild, surrounding a sun-dried lawn with a weeping willow tree in the center. Although there was no creek or river the weeping willow tree surely grew there, no doubt with the faithful reckoning that keeps some people and trees alive, waiting for the secret provision. Around the garden stood a high wall disguised and made more seemly by its dress of slow-burning ivy. I noticed that the windows of the dormitory opened casement style so that one would not have guessed they were fixed to open a limited distance; I could not see upon them the crudely nailed boards which were a feature of Cliffhaven windows. The dormitory felt cool and shaded; I could see, outside, people in sun frocks walking to and fro or sitting down in the shade of the weeping willow. The air was peaceful. There were no screams protests moanings; no sound of scuffles as a patient was forcibly persuaded to obey orders. For the people *were* patients. And it was a hospital.

Wasn't it?

I thought yes certainly it is a hospital; I had heard them say Treecroft Mental Hospital where the murderers go, this way driver.

In the bed opposite me was a woman sitting up talking to anyone who might be listening.

"I am Mrs. Ogden," she said.

Her dresses had been marked, her shoes, her nighties, and in the rush of admission they had forgotten to mark her, therefore she was telling people her name, indelibly, like the ink on the tape.

"I am Mrs. Ogden."

66

Her face had the damply absorbent pallor, her mouth the moistness with the corners drawn in, that I had seen on the consumptives at Cliffhaven. She talked breathlessly, incessantly, full of the excitement of her operation in the city where she had had a number of ribs removed. She displayed the scars. She recounted the occasion. She explained esoteric phrases of life in a general hospital.

"I was 'on hours,'" she said blissfully. "Do you know what that means? It means you are allowed up each day for so many hours. We sat around in ward chairs, in our dressing gowns. There was thunder and lightning twice and rain for a week and the rest sun. On the terrace. It's 'way out of town really. People call me Betty."

Although I could not communicate with her because I was speechless I lay in my bed, staring at her, and trying to warn her of the veneer of peace and pleasantness, the brightness of the bedspreads and the sun-frocked people outside; I tried to say beware the room is laid with traps and hung with hooks. For there was growing in my mind a dread which was not diminished but increased by the sight of the garden, the weeping willow the apparently contented patients roving freely across the sun-baked lawn. I marveled that Mrs. Ogden seemed so untroubled. How could she not know about the danger? Why did she not beware, surround herself with all possible safety measures, move lower down in her bed and draw the bedclothes up for protection?

I lay and watched the dark dread growing like one of those fairy-tale plants whose existence depends upon their lack of discipline, their uncontrolled urge to grow through and across and into and beyond until they reach the sky and block the sun. My fear crept beyond myself and into the tranquil dormitory, and turned upon me, like a child upon its parent, threatening me.

I watched the ward sister, Sister Creed, going her rounds with the doctor, speaking softly and calmly and smiling at Mrs. Ogden and myself, the only ones in bed, as a genteel hostess might welcome her guests for the week end. But as they passed nearer and walked in full view through the open door into the garden I noticed, with a feeling of alarm, that both the doctor and Sister Creed were limping. Surely it was more than coincidence! I was filled with the superstitious fear that besets primitive people and children and makes them invoke gods and repeat rhymes when faced with deformities. I was reminded of a woman we used to call the Late Lady. We used to meet her on the way to school if we were in danger of being late. "The Late Lady," we would whisper with horror in our voices and with our hearts beating fast, and with the stitch in our sides we would run for dear life to get out of sight of the limping lady and to get to school in time for the march in.

Further, the sight of the Treecroft matron convinced me that my fears were not groundless, and at first I thought that Matron Glass had followed me up from the south and adopted the identity of Matron Borough; even their bodies were the same, huge, encased in the white uniform through which you could see the marks, like bars, of their corset. Matron Borough's voice was deep and admonishing and when she looked at Mrs. Ogden and myself her expression told us that our lying in bed, putting into disarray the stiff sheets spotless from the hospital laundry, and interfering with the peaceful effect created by the rows of spruce unoccupied beds their quilts flipped exactly their castors turned at the right angle, was an affront to Ward Seven and the sooner we were "up out of that" the better.

I dreaded the moment when I should have to get dressed and stand upright buffeted by the waves in the mid-ocean of the room; and test the reality of the peace and contentment that I had observed from my bed. I could not explain my fear. What if Ward Seven were but a subaqueous condition of the mind which gave the fearful shapes drowned there a rhythmic distortion of peace; and what if, upon my getting up from my bed, the perspective was suddenly altered, or I was led into a trap where a fire burning in the walls had dried up the water and destroyed the peace by exposing in harsh daylight the submerged shapes in all their terror? How could I know?

The rule was to stay in bed for two days; I was grateful. I lay and let the doctor examine me, with the dormitory nurse modestly arranging the blankets. I made a fist, followed Dr. Tall's finger, pressed his hands away, felt the pin prick, breathed, said ninety-nine, had my knee tapped and the sole of my foot scraped. I did not ask the doctor to explain Sister Creed's limp or the startling resemblance between Matron Borough and Matron Glass of Cliffhaven; or to tell me the meaning of the weeping willow tree, the message of the mosquitoes, the bamboo, the telephoning crickets, mason flies, huhu bugs, ants that stopped in their tracks and wept if they lost their way; the great clifflike rents in the earth; the aluminium rain boiling upon the earth.

Dr. Tall was a late afternoon shadow, neat, in a white coat, with gold planted between his two front teeth; a flashy loot to which his tongue kept returning as if to make sure of its safety, or perhaps to work it loose and get rid of it like an overexposed bad habit that has lost its original delight and value.

"Do you know where you are?"

I was tempted at first to question that I was lying in Ward Seven of Treecroft Mental Hospital. Treecroft. It made me think that perhaps I had been admitted to a dove-cote. But I was speechless and only stared at Dr. Tall's gold tooth. "We'll give her E.S.T. tomorrow," he told Sister Creed.

I could not absorb any more fearful possibilities; I was so tired; if it rained, the harp hanging on the willow tree would get wet, and still I did not care. Mrs. Ogden was coughing, reaching for her sputum box and carefully measuring what she spat into it. She was flushed as if she had been making love to something or somebody that no one else could see, and she drew her breath excitedly when she saw the nurse approaching with chart and thermometer.

"It's up," she said triumphantly, as if she had won an argument with the invisible presence that seemed to attend her.

The next morning I was led with other patients in my nightgown and dressing gown into the garden and across to another ward which also opened upon the garden. I was put to bed in a room in a corridor of single rooms and told to lie there quietly and wait. I lay, tracing the pattern of the red mat on the floor, and thinking that at Cliffhaven I had never seen mats on the floors of rooms, and drowsily wondering what was going to happen to me, as if I were a threatened character in an episode of a not very gripping serial. Suddenly I heard the familiar calamitous despairing cry of a patient undergoing E.S.T., and snorting noises in the room next door, and the sound of something being wheeled along the corridor to my room.

The door opened. A strange doctor stood there with an E.S.T. machine on a trolley. He gave me a quick evil glance, approached my bed, thrust the headphones over my temples, and suddenly I was unconscious, contending alone with nightmares of grief and despair. When I woke I was led back through the garden, past the weeping willow and the empty bird bath where a few sparrows flipped themselves with dust, to peaceful Ward Seven, so peaceful that I might have wondered if the screams and the creeping machine really existed, had I not retained in my memory, as if it had entered almost without my permission, the peculiar smell of the other ward, a kind of ward body odor of polish and urine blended, in the manner of tobacco or herbs, to a compression of desolation and exuded now strongly now faintly as it was whittled, deliberately or casually, by the hanging-around corner-leaning presence that one may call Time.

In a few days I was up and dressed wandering around the ward and sitting in the garden under the willow tree and learning, as I tried to forget my still-growing disquiet and dread and the haunting smell of the other ward, as I became to all appearances one of the gentle contented patients of Ward Seven, that the E.S.T. which happened three times a week, and the succession of screams heard as the machine advanced along the corridor, were a nightmare that one suffered for one's own "good." "For your own good" is a persuasive argument that will eventually make man agree to his own destruction. I tried to reassure myself by remembering that in Ward Seven the "new" attitude ("mental patients are people like you and me") seemed to predominate the bright counterpanes, pastel-shaded walls supposed to soothe, a few abstract paintings hanging paint-in-cheek in the sitting room; tables for four in the dining room, gay with checked cloths; everything to keep up the pretense that Treecroft was a hotel, not a mental hospital, and anyway the words *mental hospital* were now frowned upon; the proper designation was now *psychiatric unit*.

The kindly Sister Creed dined with us. We had cream on our pudding, bacon and eggs for breakfast, all cooked in the ward kitchen by Hillsie, Mrs. Hill, another of the faithful long-term patients whose life is to serve. She worked from morning till late at night, though her face was always pale, her eyes cavernous and dark, and her ankles swelled at night.

"Look at my ankles," she would say.

Someone would remark, "Hillsie, you shouldn't work so hard."

"No, perhaps I shouldn't," was the answer.

But the next morning she would be up early and in the kitchen preparing breakfast, looking after the nurses with surprise cups of tea ("Hillsie, you're an angel"), scrubbing polishing. On Sundays, her only day off, when she stayed in bed all day, people would ask, with a trace of panic and irritation, "Where's Hillsie?" And on that day nothing seemed to go right, food was burnt and shriveled, utensils were lost, nobody knew where to look or how to set about doing things and Hillsie was being continually interrupted in her rest by people going to her room and demanding to know where and why and how. Hillsie's room, like Mrs. Pilling's, was decorated with pictures and calendars. She had roses from the garden in a bowl on her dressing table and a photograph of her son in his sailor's uniform, a pale handsome lad like his mother. She had been taken to Treecroft when he was born and in those days there had been no treatment for her.

On visiting days almost everyone had a visitor. An aunt decided to "adopt" me and visit me each week making a long journey by tram from the outskirts of the city. She was a middle-aged woman who had unconsciously or deliberately followed the current fashion advice that pink and gray are "right" colors for middle-aged people. She wore pink blouses and gray suits and floating chiffon scarves. Her complexion was a tinted map of red patches and vein tributaries; her eyes were vague, the whites curdled with pink like blood-specked white of egg. She was all kindness, with an intuitive knowledge of how to be a good hospital visitor—to bring comforting things to eat and after the first rather embarrassed "How are you?" which did not demand a detailed reply, sit dreamily in the garden, quiet composed uninquisitive, offering at intervals peppermint creams and fancy cakes. She expressed delight at the hospital, at the kindness of the staff, the cheerfulness of the ward, and the fact that the patients "seemed to have nothing wrong with them." One could hear other visitors making similar remarks.

"You're lucky to be here, with everybody so good. It

73

looks to me like an expensive hotel. I think I'll have a nervous breakdown myself some time. I'm only joking of course. I know what you've been through."

Most of the patients in Ward Seven liked to talk with their visitors about their "nervous breakdown," the plan of it, and details of it, as if it were a piece of property they had unexpectedly acquired. They liked to tell those nearest to them what they had "been through." And their visitors comforted them by saying, truthfully, "You'll be home soon; another few weeks and you'll be home."

And many patients did go home. There were farewells and thank yous, addresses exchanged, and promises to write, and promises to spread the news that mental hospitals were certainly not what people seemed to think, that the letters full of shocking details that appeared in the newspapers were the work of cranks and liars.

For had not the patients of Ward Seven seen for themselves the modern conditions?—that patients were regarded as human beings and cared for with kindness? Certainly shock treatment was unpleasant but after all it was for people's own good wasn't it; besides, it was held in another ward, and you were so dopey going and coming that you didn't remember much anyway. The point was that you were better and going home and you wouldn't be afraid if at any other time you had to return to Treecroft hospital.

And one day Dr. Tall said to me, too, "We'll soon have you fit and well." We saw little of him; he was always busy and only rarely found time to say "What are you knitting?" "You're doing nicely." "Hot today isn't it?" and other stagnant phrases. He cared for, or tried to care for, at least one thousand women.

74

I didn't feel ill; but I was afraid. Dr. Tall limped. Sister Creed limped. Matron Borough's butcher-like face swelled before me in a threatening manner. Yet I went obediently to the other ward, known as Ward Four-Five-and-One, for E.S.T. and tried to suppress the disquiet which amounted to panic at the distinctive ward smell, and at the very name of the ward—*Four-Five-and-One*; a sinister code no doubt; and at the sight of the ward's T.B. wing which opened off the kitchen and had a shacklike appearance with its bare wooden floors and corrugated iron roof which must have given the rooms an unbearable intensity of heat from the daylong sun, thudding like a headache in the sky. The bare floors, contrasting with the dignity and brightness of Ward Seven, depressed me, and I tried to forget them and I felt the necessity of not believing in their existence. In my mind I dare not contain an image of both Ward Seven and the Four-Five-and-One T.B. wing.

I returned with almost hysterical pleasure from the smell of desolation and the sight of the stark makeshift ward, to the supposed reality of Ward Seven and Betty Ogden's confident chatter and the fretful languor of the women gently describing their homes, their families, their symptoms, and the pleasant conditions they found in hospital. But I felt increasingly like a guest who is given every hospitality in a country mansion yet who finds in unexpected moments a trace of a mysterious presence; sliding panels; secret tappings; and at last surprises the host and hostess in clandestine conversations and plottings with mention of poison, torture, death. Or was I inhabiting, as it were, as guest for the week end, my own mind, and becoming more and more perturbed by its manifestation of evil?

75

But suddenly one evening there was a quarrel in the bathroom between Elizabeth and Mrs. Dean.

"I'm having first bath."

"No. I'm having first bath."

A mere quarrel about a bath, you will say. What is important in that, or unusual or terrifying? Few people quarreled in Ward Seven; a patient who became "uncooperative" in this respect was speedily transferred to what was called vaguely "another ward." Perhaps the argument might have died or been solved peaceably had not Matron Borough on her evening round, overheard, and opening the door of the bathroom inquired in a shocked voice, "What on earth is going on?" and stood with her fierce gaze on the half-dressed Mrs. Dean, a middle-aged woman suffering from the fact of middle age, her mind out of step with her body, nervous, worried about her appearance and her accumulation of fat and trying to tear down the signpost held before her by her age. Matron Borough's glance sent her into a fury. She began to call Matron names, to swear at her.

"You big fat bloody bullock don't you stare at me."

Matron's face and neck reddened; she too was sensitive about her appearance.

"Out of here," she said. "You ought to be ashamed of yourself. Pull yourself together. There's no excuse for your behavior."

Mrs. Dean refused to leave the bathroom. Elizabeth was standing by, subdued, a picture of cooperation.

"Right," snapped Matron, beckoning to a nurse; and moving towards the door in the bathroom which was always kept locked and which I had never seen used, Matron Borough opened it, and with the three other nurses who

76

had arrived, dragged the struggling Mrs. Dean through the door.

She never returned to the ward.

I brooded upon this mysterious disappearance. Where had she gone? To "another ward"?

Then one day, in recognition of the fact that I was getting well and would soon be allowed out, a nurse asked me to accompany her to the "big kitchen" to return the porridge can—the porridge was the only food not cooked by Hillsie. I had never seen beyond the Ward Seven garden, and I gazed about me, asking questions, and expressing surprise that the hospital was such an extensive place. Seen from the outside, from beyond the genteel front entrance where it looked like an ivy-covered mansion, it was a number of sprawling dilapidated buildings; the big kitchen squat and dirty in appearance stood opposite a ward that seemed in such a state of decay that I asked its name.

"What's that place?"

"Oh that? Lawn Lodge."

We entered the poorly lit poorly ventilated kitchen, and were immediately surrounded by the smell of boiled cabbage. We passed a vat which bubbled with greasy meat, and another where a thick mess of farina was cooking, watched over by a hairy-chested man in an open-necked check shirt. He suddenly thrust his hairy arm into the vat of farina and began stirring vigorously. I was amazed, and impressed, and eager to get back to reassure myself that our ward meals were cooked by Hillsie, indeed that Ward Seven was still in existence. Returning past the conglomeration of old buildings which seemed unreal in their lack of relationship to our bright admission ward, we met two attendants carrying out the back way from Four-Five-and-One, a corpse, bloated-looking under its canvas.

"That's Mrs. Dean," the nurse said indiscreetly. "She died."

I was glad to return to Ward Seven and try to convince myself that the garden, the lawn, the weeping willow, the windows and doors wide open, were not a dream, and that Treecroft, even if some of its buildings appeared antiquated, was a hospital with a modern attitude to mental illness. But I was attacked increasingly by disquiet; I had seen, as it were, the sliding panels, overheard the sinister conversation.

I I

I CONTINUED TO HAVE E.S.T., dreading more and more the sound of the trolley and the stifled screams as it moved from room to room, nearer and nearer. And suddenly the brightness of Ward Seven seemed to burst into a glare of chaotic vegetation, as if it existed now merely to camouflage the movements of deadly reptiles and poisonous insects. I heard the nurses speaking sharply, threateningly. At mealtimes now the check tableclothes startled me; they seemed striped with blood and disaster. No one suspected the growing danger. I noticed other doors besides the mysterious one in the bathroom; and I had no means of finding where they led, although once there was a door opened into another ward and the sour smell of wet bedclothes seeped through and mingled with the heavy sweetness of the arum lilies on the mantelpiece, the Christmas lilies that relatives use at funerals to hide the smell of death.

It was late summer now with explosions of thunder that almost cracked our bones and vivid graphs of lightning scrawled in the sky. The birdbath in the garden overflowed with warm steamy rain, the soaked slender leaves of the

79

weeping willow drooped, burned at the edges and the tips, like soft green curls of paper held to a flame and drawn swiftly away. And we sat inside in the supposedly friendly room. Slowly, twitching a muscle, refocusing a malevolent gaze, the insects moved across the carpet and the reptiles slid through the pastel-shaded slime of the walls, their tongues darting and devouring.

And now, when Aunt Rose came to visit me, I was yet more silent, and helped myself more feverishly to peppermint creams and fancy cakes. Our wooden seat under the willow tree was battered and blood stained; people were digging graves on the lawn in the night; tiny lizards with brown corrugated faces came from the door of Four-Five-and-One and snapped up the sun and disappeared, their throats knocking.

"It's so peaceful here," said Aunt Rose.

It began to snow.

"Soon," the doctor repeated, "we'll have you fit and well."

He also did not seem to be aware of the mysterious processions of the lights the crepe and calico circles the white weave the sprocket conforming the throne mutinous and the moss-grown faces and the fingerprints ah the fingerprints of swift click and light, the secret camera.

I grew more frightened. I began to wander in the night and to panic at mealtimes, faced with the squares of blood and the bone china—why was it bone? I tried to understand what was happening. When the door to the other ward was sometimes opened I tried to realize the juxtaposition of Ward Seven and Ward Six where, crowded bed to bed, the old women lay with dropped jaws and hollow cheeks and hands fretting at the bedclothes. I tried to fathom the smell of hopelessness that seeped through, tainting our furniture and carpets and cushions, and the smell I brought back with me from Four-Five-and-One, as if I had been visiting a temple where a mixture of loneliness and despair was burned in place of incense.

One morning I saw that the nurse had collected my clothes and was checking them with the official list.

"You're going to another ward," she said.

My heart almost stopped. I felt my face grow pale.

"Where?"

"Oh, only next door. Four-Five-and-One."

I STOOD IN THE dayroom of Four-Five-and-One. It was deserted except for a midget woman sitting sewing, her legs dangling from the battered leather sofa which with the other shabby furniture reminded me of the old-fashioned waiting room at Mr. Peters', our family dentist; and looking up at the walls I expected to see the familiar faded photograph of the club First Eleven, sitting with their legs and arms crossed, with the youthful clean-shaven Mr. Peters cradling the football between his knees and staring belligerently from the center of the front row. But there were no pictures or photographs on the wall. And gradually the characteristic ward smell, like something brewed in the floor and the walls and the furniture, leaked out and filled the room with such stifling force that had it been smoke there would have been cries of Fire, Fire, and attempts to escape from suffocation. But what warning do you cry for a smell that, as much as fire and smoke, has a capacity to destroy?

The midget woman worked busily at her tablecloth, and I knew from the intricacy of the pattern and the care with which it was being followed, that this woman had been in hospital a long time. I had seen it before, at Cliffhaven, this needling of their whole life into a piece of fancywork —a dressing-table cover, caddy, tablecloth; with no hope of ever seeing it in their own home, on their own furniture. They worked with the evolvement and detachment of true artists; one could see how they cared for something that would be sold or given away and soiled into anonymity; how they folded it neatly into the small bag where they kept their treasures. The midget woman had just such a small bag beside her. It held a magazine, knitting patterns, wool, needles, perhaps something to eat or a squashed chocolate at the bottom, or something picked up, that others might consider a trifle, but which she valued enough to keep and be unwilling, even roused to anger, if asked to discard. I stood alone by the door, near the piano with its lid up showing its uncleaned loose teeth wedged into gums of musty green baize, strengthening the impression suggested by the furniture—an obscenity of dental decay, waiting rooms, dreariness. I waited for the appearance of someone other than the midget woman. It occurred to me that in all my visits to Four-Five-and-One I had seen few patients belonging to the ward. Did they hide in burrows? Did they live in the wall and emerge only at mealtime? Or were they perpetually immured, and the smell that oozed from the wood was their personal smell of imprisonment that drained through their skin and their mind and their whole body?

The dayroom door was not locked; yet I was afraid to move. I stood shivering in the corner, and trying to understand the meaning of being in Four-Five-and-One. I dared not go outside in the garden and face the curious questions

83

and glances of the privileged Ward Seven patients; nor could I go to the room where I was now to sleep, at the end of the corridor where E.S.T. was given. I stood all afternoon in the sunless dayroom. Occasionally the midget woman gave a cluck of excitement when she concluded a rose or perfected a spray of leaves, and she held her embroidery at arm's length to get the general effect. Once I surprised her doing nothing, her work fallen as if she really did not care about it or were persuading herself not to care, her eyes staring with a grim expression and a frown on her face, which was freckled and aged, as is the way with midgets, when their features seem to bear a double burden of time that would in normal growth be carried by their changing and developing body.

Suddenly, from somewhere in the ward, a deep gong boomed again and again and immediately the whole ward seemed to come alive, as if the sound had disturbed the patients, like insects or flightless birds from their nests, and I saw people small tall fat thin deformed mongoloid dwarfed appearing as if from nowhere from corners and hiding places, and with their little bags of treasures in their hands, hurrying and scurrying in obedience to the gong. I followed them. I arrived with them at the dining room and, following their example, queued outside the servery. I could see beyond the ward kitchen the T.B. wing and the dismal bare floors of its corridor and a feeling of desolation overcame me. Nurses were shouting orders. People were being reprimanded. Everyone, plate in hand, was hastening to her table, triumphant in the knowledge of where to go and what to do.

I burst into tears and fled from the room. I was fetched

back forcibly by a nurse and sat at one of the tables and my meal was put before me. The desolation flowed around me and through me and caught in my throat so that I could not make the movements necessary for eating food. I sat listening to the excited irritated chatter of Four-Five-and-One. I heard the words "laundry" "sewing room" and gossip connected with these, and guessed that Four-Five-and-One were the workers of the hospital; their conversation was that of a people who had had an unaltered way of life for many years and who expected, indeed desired, that it should continue. I heard no one, as in Ward Seven, talking of their families or their nervous breakdown and its symptoms; it was obvious that eccentricity was either not realized or else accepted, as the way of life in the ward, and certainly not discussed.

There seemed a haste, an urgency about everything, and tea was quickly finished and the knives counted, and there was a feeling in the air that the most important events of the day were about to occur. The dining room was quickly emptied. I noticed one of the patients who had left her bag behind come running back for it with panic in her eyes until she found it hadn't been stolen. A half-eaten apple rolled from the top; swiftly she retrieved it, stuffing it into her bag. Then she went upstairs in the direction of the big dormitories where apparently most of the patients slept; perhaps she would rummage around in her locker, arranging things, or, as was the habit of many of us, stand for a few moments beside her bed, as if affirming her claim to it. I tried to go along the corridor to visit my own room, to touch the bed and walk from corner to corner, but I was told, "Dayroom. No one in the corridor until bedtime."

I returned to the dayroom which was beginning now to be crowded with people bustling in expectantly as if to attend an eventful rally. People sat busily sewing knitting quarreling talking, occasionally glancing up and staring with eager anticipation at the door. A radio on a high caged shelf, tuned to the local commercial station, let out a blare of singing commercials about toothpaste razor blades soap; a nurse unlocked the radio and switched it off and immediately there were complaints and loud cries of dissent.

At intervals a patient fell to the floor in a fit.

"It's Marjorie again," someone would say. Or Nancy. Or Pamela. And her bag would be guarded for her until she came to and reached out for it, confusedly exploring to see that nothing had been interfered with or stolen.

And all evening the air of expectancy persisted; whatever these people were waiting for, they were content to wait with little spurts of excitement at times when it seemed that the longed-for event was about to occur. Bedtime came. There was further fuss and flurry and eager adventurous progress along corridors and up staircases; high-pitched voices seeming unable to bear the excitement of knowing that surely whatever was going to happen would happen soon, soon. And if not tonight why not tomorrow? Or the day after? I was ushered along the corridor and locked in my room, and my clothes tied by the sleeves of my cardigan and left outside the door; and sleep came in without knocking.

The days passed. At mealtimes I sat at my place at the table, without eating, for the ward smell and the strangeness so overcame me and soaked into me that the food and the air and the people tasted of it. And the people: I knew now that they were automatons geared to a pitch of excitement they could not understand and fearful lest whatever or whoever controlled them should tire of giving them distraction, and let them run down like broken toys and have to find in their own selves a way of overcoming the desolation in which they lived. And after a month, and little food, I had grown so thin that I was put to bed, indefinitely, to rest; and I lay there apathetically, being fed rice and scrambled eggs.

They thought I was ill. What would they have said if I had told them that illness can be caused by a smell, that it was the smell of Four-Five-and-One which was draining all my energy and desire to live? I could not escape from it; I was surrounded by it. And it could not seem to be that people lived in this way, like the patients of Four-Five-and-One, crowded and lonely, unvisited, going sometimes in a bus or as a worker's privilege to a picnic; involved in their way of life as the only way they had known for years and would know now until they died. It could not seem to be that Four-Five-and-One opened on to the garden, sharing the birdbath and the weeping willow and the dropping roses with the gentle patients of Ward Seven who reclined in their bright "contemporary" sitting-room in gaily covered chairs and had delicious finically cooked meals, with cream and second helpings.

I was not surprised when one of the Four-Five-and-One patients, Mrs. Jopson, who had evidently become separated from the sustaining concerted eagerness of the ward, jumped from the fire escape one day and killed herself.

One morning, without my having suspected anything beforehand, I was given E.S.T. And when I woke I was given it again. When I saw the machine approaching for the second time I lost all control of myself in a culminating panic of screaming, and when I woke then, I saw the nurse arranging my clothes in a neat pile on the chair by the bed.

"You're going to another ward," she told me.

I was exhausted and not very curious but I asked, "Where?"

"Lawn Lodge."

IV

*W*HEN THE NURSE delivered me at the door of Lawn Lodge she cautioned the nurse receiving me, "Watch out. She'll fly at you."

I had never shown aggression; I had never "flown" at anyone. I had been only frightened confused and depressed and my appetite had decayed at the mercy of the powerful ward smell, like fresh meat exposed to the sun and the flies. For it was true—the smell had been like the sun, in that the world of Four-Five-and-One revolved round it and drew from it a desolate kind of life; and the smell was like the flies the way it sucked at the air and at our breaths and our clothes and the invisible apparel of our minds. And now I was in Lawn Lodge, the refractory ward, in a room full of raging screaming fighting people, a hundred of them, many in soft strait jackets, others in long canvas jackets that fastened between the thighs, with the crossed arms laced at the back with stiff cord, and no way out for the hands. At one end of the long dismal room was a heavy table, split and seamed with dirt, where about sixteen people sat with one nurse to guard them: this was the "special" table, and the patients sitting here were not allowed to move from their places all day until they were driven along the corridor to bed. I was put at the special table next to Piona, an ex-Borstal girl, who had had a brain operation and was wearing a soft jacket of ticking.

"What do you fink," she said—she could not pronounce "th"—"What do you fink? Once here you never get out."

I watched from the special table, as from a seat in a concert hall, the raging mass of people performing their violent orchestration of unreason that seemed like a new kind of music of curse and cry with the undertone of silence flowing from the quiet ones, the curled-up, immovable and nameless; and the movement was a ballet, and the choreographer was Insanity; and the whole room seemed like a microfilm of atoms in prison dress revolving and voyaging, if that were possible, in search of their lost nucleus.

Two patients attacked each other murderously. I was horrified to feel in myself the communal excitement that spread through the patients and the three nurses at the prospect of a tooth-and-claw battle. I was more horrified to see that, at times, the nurses tried to provoke the patients into displays of violence. They did this with Helen who walked stiffly like a tin soldier, holding her arms out as if to embrace anyone who came her way, and whispering, "Love, Love," in a manner that would have been banal in a Hollywood film but here seemed pitiful and real.

"Love me, Helen," the nurse would call, and Helen smiling with anticipated joy, would advance carefully towards the nurse only to be turned aside with a scornful remark when her arms had almost encircled their longed-for objective of flesh. Her love changed to hate then; she would attack, and the nurse would blow her whistle bringing other nurses to her aid, and Helen would be put in a strait jacket and for the rest of the day would rage about the room using her feet, her shoes having been removed, to convey her anger and frustration.

Day after day from my seat at the special table I watched the baiting of Helen.

Soon the seething whole began to take shape as individuals—there was the Queen of Norway, a charming middle-aged woman with a serene face and beautiful bronze-colored hair wound in plaits like a crown about her head. When she was questioned by the delighted nurses who loved her and liked to keep her in conversation about her palace, her servants, her sovereignty, she would smile a sweet dimpled smile and in her "Norwegian" accent, let her imagination rove. And there was Milty, another favorite, a tall athletic woman with an engaging personality and a facility for finding cigarette butts and transforming them into smokeable cigarettes. She spent her day waltzing, with one of the ghosts that are easy to conjure, when one is ill, held lovingly in her arms. And moving in dignity around the room—bestowing now always welcome blessings, turning a prophetic gaze upon the vision of squalor and agitation that surrounded her—a white-haired Christ walked up and down, confined and restless. She prayed. And she wept. And she flew to attack when they tried to restore to Milty the cigarette butt which Christ had snatched during her ministrations.

But among those with interesting delusions and those who were pointed out by the nurses with awe because they had committed murder (the hospital was known as the "safest" in the country, for murderers) there was the majority whose only recognizable claim to personality was their name, itself often almost forgotten and replaced by a nickname; there were the irritating self-centered epileptics who quarreled with everybody and were shown no sympathy; the proud suspicious patients aloof from the others in a private grandeur which, had they been willing to share it with the nurses, would have brought them interested attention, perhaps an occasional cigarette more than their ration, or a sweet for being "so quaint, such a darling." And there were the people who had long ago given up attempts at speech and now made noises more appropriate to their habitat: animal noises, whimpers; sometimes they bayed and howled like lonely dogs attending the moon. Others were dumb, retreating entirely, curled up all day, unmoving, under the long tables that were used for meals and afterwards pushed back against the wall.

Four-Five-and-One had oppressed with its desolation; here in Lawn Lodge I was so shocked that for a time I felt emotionally blindfolded, trying to find my way among unrecognizable feelings and being given no help by former familiar landmarks that seemed now to have their shape disguised, to be deliberately pointing me to confusion.

I could not believe Lawn Lodge. I wanted the peeled layers of human dignity to be restored, as in one of those trick films where the motion moves backwards, so that I could not see beneath the surface.

I stayed at the special table for some weeks. The "jackets," twenty-four of them, had a table to themselves; all had to be fed. The silent ones also were fed, their throats massaged to make them swallow. For the rest of us meals were a bedlam of grabbing and throwing and almost delirious excitement, especially when the supply of sausages or saveloys would finish before the last table had been served and a mutinous hungry mob had to be calmed with concessional phrases like "We'll serve you first tomorrow" or "We'll give you two sausages next time"; for enough food was never sent to us from the big kitchen.

Sitting at the special table we had the luxury of always being served first and therefore did not suffer if any mistakes were made in the calculation of the size of helpings or if the "big kitchen" (it was referred to as a culpable being) did not send enough trays.

Sometimes, with our share of stodgy apple pie in front of us, we were seized with an unreal extravagance and exuberance and would suddenly hurl our meal in the air and onto the wall behind us where it stuck and stained. This desperate rejection of what was so dear to us was infectious, as is self-sacrifice in wartime. I joined in the throwing of the food; Piona and Sheila, another ex-Borstal girl and I were accurate markswomen, breaking off precious breadcrumbs from our too-small slice of bread, and flicking them about the table, at the nurses and the other patients. We would have aimed at the doctor too but he did not pass through the Lawn Lodge dayroom. We flicked; we banged our crockery on the table; we sang rude rhymes about "I took my girl to the pictures and sat her in the stalls and every time the lights went out . . ."

And nearly every moment of every day I remembered what Piona had said: "What do you fink? You stay in Lawn Lodge for ever."

Our sleeping quarters were divided into two downstairs dormitories both locked, crowded with beds placed head to foot and side by side with scarcely room to undress. There were no lockers or any places to keep possessions, if we had been allowed any. For those who were thought to need them, there were single rooms along the corridor, downstairs, and upstairs where there were also two open dormitories for the reliable patients. At first I slept in one of the locked dormitories, the foot of my bed reaching the head of Barbara's bed. Barbara did not sleep all night. She sat up in bed rubbing her hands together and giggling.

Very soon, because of my habit of wandering in the night, I was transferred to a room along the corridor downstairs. In the morning all patients from the dormitories and rooms were crowded into the tiny washroom to be dressed. There was little hope of washing, and as one entered the room one was bulldozed as it were by the smell of stale bodies. We stood there naked, packed tightly like cattle at the saleyards, and awaiting the random distribution of our clothes which usually arrived with one or two articles missing. I was shocked once to find myself without pants. I made a fuss. I was becoming adept at making a fuss, at arguing and trying to stand up for my rights and the rights of the other patients whom I felt the responsibility of protecting. I complained loudly, "I've got no pants."

"Pants?" exclaimed Sister Wolf who was small lithe and sharp tongued, with an exposed rocklike face covered daily with heavy make-up which served, I suppose, the same purpose as lichen. "What do you want with pants? There are no men around."

That was true. The only men we saw were the stubble-faced kitchen men who came to the door with blackened trays of sausages or stew.

So I went without pants and sometimes without stockings, and I dreaded every month when I would have to ask for sanitary napkins which were supplied by the hospital, for once or twice I was refused them, and told by the overworked besieged staff, "Use your arse hole." In the end I did not seem to care; and if I wanted to go to the lavatory from the special table, and I was often wanting to go, and I was refused permission, I would slide from my seat under the table and wet on the floor like an animal.

It was winter now and cold, for there was no heating in the building; and sometimes it rained all day and we could hear the water splashing in the puddles and gurgling in the spouting, but we could not see, for the lower part of the windows was boarded up, like in a house visited by the plague. I thought of Ward Seven, its brightness and kindness and the gently melancholy patients talking of their aches and pains and not being able to sleep and suffering all the sweet irritations of consciousness; talking too of home and relatives and plans for the future; everything seeming so tidy and certain and safe. I remembered the weeping willow, and the harp now destroyed by frost and damp; and Sister Creed limping about the pastel-walled rooms arranging the gay tablecloths smoothing the cheerful counterpanes. And the days passed packing and piling themselves together like sheets of absorbent material, deadening the sound of our lives, even to ourselves, so that perhaps if a tomorrow ever came it would not hear us; its new days would bury us, in its own name; we would be like people entombed when the rescuers, walking about in the dark waving lanterns and calling to us, eventually give up because no one answers them; sometimes they dig, and find the victims dead. So time was falling upon us, like snow, muffling our cries and our lives, and who would melt it for us?

> *White bird featherless*
> *Flew down from Paradise*
> *Pitched on the castle wall.*
> *Along came Lord Landless*
> *Took it up handless*
> *Rode with it horseless*
> *To the King's White Hall.*

Would it help if we crossed our hands on our breasts and spoke riddles?

V

ONE DAY I WAS moved from the special table and became a member of the "rest" surging about in the dayroom. I was afraid. I sat on one of the long wooden forms and turned to face Betty who sat on the other end. I smiled at her. I hoped that my smile showed love and a desire to help her. Suddenly I received a heavy blow from her fist, right on my nose, and my eyes filled with tears that began as tears of pain but ended in tears of hopelessness and loneliness: how could I help them if they were going to hit me? A nurse came up to me.

"That's Betty's seat. Nobody sits on that form but Betty. She's homicidal."

"Why didn't you tell me?" I asked.

"Oh. I wanted to see what would happen," was the candid reply. "Don't take it badly. It's all in a day's fun. Here, join the lolly scramble."

The lolly scramble was a feature of some days and was held both for the amusement of the staff who often described themselves as "going dippy ourselves, stuck on duty here all day" and for the pleasure of the patients. The nurses, feeling bored because there hadn't been a recent fight, would fetch a bag of sweets from the tin which was bought ever fortnight as part of the Social Security allowance for the patients. The paper lollies would be showered into the middle of the dayroom and it would be first come first served with fights developing, people being put in strait jackets, whistles blowing; and the tension which mounted and reached its peak at intervals—both in the patients and in the nurses who had long ago had to suppress any desire to 'nurse' and were now overworked degraded, in many case sadistic, custodians—found its release, for a time.

After a lolly scramble, when the fights had been dealt with, there was unusual quietness and dreaminess and sometimes laughter, and those who had been successful in the rush held tight to their sweet sticky booty. The toffees always had the same taste, of dark swampy syrup that made one feel sick and at the same time gave comfort. Although I longed to, I never joined the scramble, and viewing it from the outside, was filled with disgust that the staff had so far forgotten that the people in their charge were human beings, as to treat them like animals in a pen at the zoo.

My own taste for toffees came at night when, being hurried along the corridor to bed, I felt such pangs of hunger that I became skillful at darting unobserved into the open pantry, and sometimes snatching a handful of toffees from a newly opened tin. But that was a rare occasion. More often I seized in one hand a slice of bread from the bin and delved honey from a large tin, pasting it, ants and all, with my fingers across the bread, and thrusting the whole in the sweaty hairy hollow under my arm, and withdrawing it and eating it, salt and sweet and gritty, in the quiet of my room.

My room had no shutter. I could see the sky at night and down below a puddle-filled enclosure outside a brick building from which came the sound of an engine shunting and tides falling upon the beach, as if a private ferry were in operation with the bodies being taken from shore to shore. But my stay in my room, though not my secret gorgings of bread and honey was abruptly ended when, one evening as I lay in bed, I heard sinister whispering outside my door. I had been unusually difficult that day in obeying orders, had "talked back" to the nurses, had screamed out of hopelessness; and now I was apprehensive, wondering what my punishment would be. The voices continued their whispering.

"We'll give her shock treatment tomorrow," one said. "A worse shock than she's ever had; and she can't escape. You've locked the door securely?"

"Yes," replied the other. "She's down for shock. It will put her in her place I tell you. She needs to be taught a lesson. No breakfast for her tomorrow."

"No breakfast," the other voice repeated. "She's for shock."

My heart beat fast so that I found it hard to breathe; I was overcome by such a feeling of panic that although it seemed like breaking and distorting the only image of sky that was left to me, I smashed the window with my fist, to get out or to get at the glass and destroy myself to prevent the coming of tomorrow and the dreaded E.S.T.

For gone now were the old "brave" days at Cliffhaven when I had preserved enough calm to queue for treatment and to watch the beds with the unconscious patients in them, being wheeled from the treatment room. Ever since the morning in Four-Five-and-One when they had surprised me by giving me two consecutive treatments, although I had been given no more, and although, as I learned, I had been transferred to Lawn Lodge because they could "do nothing with me," I still lived in dread of the morning when the door would be unlocked and the nurse would greet me with, "No breakfast for you this morning. Keep on your nightgown and your dressing gown. You're for treatment."

Hearing the commotion of breaking glass the nurse hurried to the room and burst in, and I was put into the opposite room which was dark and shuttered, and I climbed shivering between the cold stiff sheets made colder by the mackintosh under them, and uncomfortable by the stalks of straw sticking through the mattress. I was given paraldehyde and slept.

The next morning my fear returned, yet I found out that I had been mistaken, that I was not "for treatment."

I could no longer control my fear; it persisted and grew stronger and day after day I made myself a nuisance by asking, asking, asking if they were planning to give me E.S.T. or to do anything terrible to me, to bury me alive in a tunnel in the earth so that no matter how long I called for help no one would hear me, to remove part of my brain and turn me into a strange animal who had to be led about with a leather collar and chain and wearing a striped dress.

And now whenever I saw the Matron and Sister Wolf talking together I suffered agonies of suspense. I knew they were talking about me; they were planning to murder me with electricity, to send me to Mount Eden Prison where I would be hanged at daybreak. Sometimes I screamed at

Matron and Sister to stop their conversation; sometimes now I attacked the nurses because I knew they were hiding the truth from me, refusing to tell me the fearful plans they were making. And I had to know. I had to know. How else could I make arrangements to protect myself, to gather all the devices for use in extreme emergency and take things calmly so that I would know which to use? If only there had been someone to tell me!

I would have asked the assurance of the doctor but where was he? It was well known that Lawn Lodge patients were "so far gone" that it was not much use the doctor devoting his valuable time to them, that it was wiser for him to be attending the others, the Ward Seven and the convalescent people who could be "saved." Only once I saw the doctor pass through the dayroom of Lawn Lodge. He limped quickly from door to door. On his face was an expression of horror and fear that changed to incredulity as if he were saying to himself, "It is not so. I am a young enthusiastic doctor, only a few years out of medical school. I live with my wife and child across the road in the house provided for me. My God what means the hospitality of the soul?"

VI

FEW VISITORS CAME, a faithful little group with their thermos flasks and their string bags of delicacies, to perform the tender resigned communication by cake and biscuit and sweet, where the habit of speech had long ago lapsed. One visiting afternoon immediately after lunch, when the tables were pushed back against the wall and we began once again our prowling up and down the worn wooden floor or sat, knees up, giving incredible puppet shows, on the tables, an enclosure of wooden forms was built near the door leading to the corridor and into the visiting room.

Those assessed as likely to have visitors (after a humiliating scrutiny with comments like "Jane? Oh not her. Nobody comes to see her." "Dora? There might be someone. Usually they don't bother. Mary? She's never had a visitor in all the time I've been here. Frankie? Maybe.") were brought beyond the enclosure, like cattle chosen for exhibit, to wait for the dressing operations which began when two nurses entered dragging a sheeted bundle. The knots were untied and "best" clothes, anybody's clothes as long as they nearly fitted, lay ready to be put on anybody. The waiting patients were already being stripped of their high-waisted faded floral smocks and subjected to a swift curry-combing process with a damp flannel and a ward comb. Shoes were put on, ward shoes, black lace-ups with a dusty shine on them, and there were high-spirited clompings up and down and attempts at skating and kicking. A pillowcase of garters was emptied on the floor and distributed with earnest persuasions not to ping them but to wear them for keeping up stockings.

Some patients had gray ward socks; others whose relatives had remembered that mentally sick people, at least on gala occasions like visiting day, may sometimes wear the kind of clothes worn in the outside world, had their own real nylons, pulled delicately and dangled from smooth cellophane envelopes. What did it matter that, after visiting hours, those same nylons would be ruined? While the dressing operation continued for the few patients, the majority beyond the sacred enclosure behaved almost as usual, giving little intimation that they knew or cared that for an hour their companions would be making a brief contact with the outside world and returning flushed baffled inclined to violence with a handful of perishable trophies got from their bewildering safari in the long-abandoned maze of human communication. There was annoyance though at the way the enclosure forced some patients to change their habitual route round and round the room; some panicked, like ants when the scent of their track is broken; others paid no heed at all.

Or so it would seem; unless one realized that the streamlined insanity of their behavior was the product, in the beginning, of crude longing dug out from their heart.

Aunt Rose was my constant visitor. There was a drawing room powder-puff air about her that made it hard for me to realize that she was my aunt; she seemed more to belong to other children; for you see I felt myself to be a child. I was so glad to see her. We sat in a dining room belonging to an adjoining ward while Sister Wolf sat in command at a special table in the front of the room, looking vigilantly about her and sometimes uttering a peremptory "Quiet please." This brought fear to the faces of the visitors who were after all to be pitied, as emotion could still write fitting signals on their faces and they had not learned to apply the mask of nothingness. Their faces showed fear, loneliness, exasperation, resignation, sympathy; looking from visitor to patient you could not tell immediately which was which until you tracked down the "set" look in the face and body of the patient, as if her whole being, like a human jelly, had been poured into the mold of Lawn Lodge.

Aunt Rose would be waiting timidly at her seat, as far away as possible from the ward sister. Although I tried hard to be polite, as soon as I had arrived and received her damp strawberry-smelling kiss, I would look at her bag and not be able to keep my eyes off it, wondering what she had brought me. She understood and immediately unpacked, as from a Christmas stocking, a supply of food for us to eat together, she taking her time and nibbling daintily while I devoured hungrily and with secret shame at my greed.

One day she brought me a bag she had sewn for me. "To put your things in," she said. It was pink cretonne with a drawstring and roses round the top in a border and a circular base of cardboard; and my hand going into it was like a bee entering a flower. I was so proud of it. I knew I would have to guard it carefully. I had not the heart to tell Aunt Rose that perhaps it might be taken from me, labeled, and put in the suitcase room to be collected by myself when I left the hospital or, as Lawn Lodge was generally accepted to be "for ever," by my sister or Aunt Rose herself when I died and word was sent for someone to remove my "things." Yet I hoped to keep it by me, for I had seen one or two people who lived upstairs, clutching little bags, but not ones like mine, not with roses round the top and a drawstring.

The bag was like my final entry paper into the land of the lost people. I was no longer looking from the outside on the people of Four-Five-and-One and their frightening care for their slight store of possessions; I was now an established citizen with little hope of returning across the frontier; I was in the crazy world, separated now by more than locked doors and barred windows from the people who called themselves sane.

I had a pink cretonne bag to put my treasures in.

It rained for weeks. When the men came to the door delivering the trays from the big kitchen they stood in puddles of water and the rain dripped from their oilskin capes. We were cold hungry and bored and fought now and again to liven things up, though I never fought with the patients for I regarded it as my duty to protect them from unkindness and it distressed me when the nurse, to excuse words that to an ordinary person would be hurting and cruel, said, "She doesn't know any better. She doesn't know what I'm saying. Can't you understand that these people to all intents and purposes are dead?"

It may seem strange to learn that all the nurses were most of the time without compassion; until one remembers that those who longed to care for their patients either gave up their lonely struggle in its unfavorable conditions of staff shortages and twelve-hour days, or were corrupted into harassed reluctant hypocrites and bullies with some sweet talk in Ward Seven and coarse instances in Lawn Lodge.

After days of rain suddenly the weather cleared and we were turned out of the stinking dayroom into the small yard downstairs, and stood shivering in the washed blue air or sat on the railing of the dilapidated veranda and looked at the yacht-filled harbor and the dark-blue patches of deep water and the pearl-colored shallows, and the snail-curled pattern of the mud flats at dead low water. I remember the idyllic songs my mother used to compose about this northern harbor that she had never seen. "Sailing down the Waitemata" and the sight of the mud flats made me homesick for all the times I had stood on beaches when the tide was out and the shadows of the clouds moved across the herringbone patterns on the sand, and I dug with my toes for clams and cockles.

Sometimes, from the seat on the railing which I shared with Piona and Sheila, we saw men patients, and hailed them unashamedly with bawdy phrases and comments on our lovely legs; or we were silent, just being Lawn Lodge people and knowing there was no hope for us. And it was cold. Sometimes I had no pants on or no shoes and stockings because when my bundle was given out in the morning they were missing and there was no time, in the rush of dressing one hundred people, to attend to the needs of those who, like myself, were capable of dressing unaided.

I sat on the veranda or hobbled about the yard, for I had an infected foot; many people had infected limbs and there was a constant going and coming on the battered wooden stairs to have our bandages fixed and our injections of penicillin. I belonged now to the raging mass of people and the dead lying, like rests in the music, upon the ground. I knew the mad language which created with words, without using reason, has a new shape of reason; as the blind fashion from touch an effective shape of the sight denied them. I knew that the people about me dared to believe what few others are even half afraid to suspect; that things are not what they seem. I knew that the dark-haired quiet woman who peered through a separated plank in the fence at the workmen digging the deep clay ditches to repair the drains was watching the digging of her own grave. And that when a nurse came to fetch Maria because an unexpected visitor had called, to Maria there was no visitor. Her arms were scarred where she had been tortured in the concentration camp in Europe; her mind was more scarred. She knew little English. Although I learned to say to her in Yugoslav, Hello, We are your friends, You have a nice smile; and the nurses, moved by the novelty of her foreignness and the indisputable appalling evidence of her body scars, at first addressed her kindly and tried to calm her, nothing seemed to help her; not when every summons to go upstairs meant a last visit to the torture or the gas chamber.

Although I was capable of what I think was "sensible" conversation there were few people to talk to and in approaching anyone it was necessary to adopt a similar mental disguise—like the soldiers who wear branches in their hats in order to harmonize with the surrounding vegetation and allay the suspicions of the enemy. But are not those the tactics that all people use when they try to emerge from themselves and engage in the perils of human communciation? I talked to Piona who could neither read nor write and found it hard to match her ideas with speech as if every time she wanted to say something, to emerge from herself, it was like trying to open a door and being prevented by great masses of dullness like the rubble of toppled buildings pressing down and entombing her; and she would retreat inside and give up trying to get out by way of speech. She found it easier to throw things, to chant swear words, and make sounds and giggles that did not have any obvious meaning yet were full of meaning; as if she had found a way of sending out signals from her buried room.

And I talked with Sheila, the other ex-Borstal girl, a quick-witted twice-married once-divorced matron of twenty. Sheila had mysterious contacts with the men patients. One day she proudly confided to me that in the toe of her shoe she had six and fourpence and a key fashioned by one of the men in the machine shop and delivered to her by the kitchen man when he brought the stew. I wished her well in her escape. That night she accomplished the old prison trick of packing her bed with bedclothes in human shape, and the next morning she was gone. The papers carried the usual headlines—I imagine they did because I did not see them—MENTAL PATIENT ESCAPES; and people out in the world locked their doors at night and in the daytime gathered to complain about the carelessness of the authorities and the lack of security precautions at the largest mental hospital in the country where "it is well known that the most desperate murderers are held"; and letters appeared in the newspapers saying it was time something "was done" and "how can an ordinary citizen expect to walk through the streets at night with lunatics at large."

Sheila was caught, along with the man, the "dangerous patient" who had escaped with her. She was put in seclusion where she sang happily, "Sweet violets, sweeter than the roses," and "Po kare kare ana" and communicated with Piona who was locked upstairs, having become uncontrollable in Sheila's absence, by beating a tattoo on her bedstead. The doctor came to visit her, a rare privilege. She charmed him, cadged a packet of smokes from him, and he went away smiling and saying to the nurse, "Give the little dear a dose of paraldehyde. She simply loves the stuff."

A week later Sheila suffered a hemorrhage of the kidneys, and a fortnight later she was dead, and the men came in the middle of the night to remove her body in the covered-wagon stretcher.

One stopped only momentarily for death; just the slight pause and panic that lie in the gap between heartbeats.

I did not talk to Louise; I listened to her. "You know," she said, demonstrating with her hands, "we have miles and miles of intestines."

"Three hundred miles to be exact."

I had a vision of those diagrams of tightly packed tubes which appear in advertisements for liver medicines and constipation cures, and I was not surprised that Louise was haunted by the plumbing of the human body, so much that it occupied her thoughts to the point of insanity. At night she could not sleep for thinking of the maze of intestines and the obstinacy of the waste forcing its way out. She was concerned too, she told me, that a drop of acid was enough to "burn the lining of the stomach, eat through the wall." I gave a shudder at the thought of the apparent blowtorch effect, the oxyacetylene gear that lay in our stomachs; I guessed that Louise was living in a horror story more alarming than any found in science-fiction paperbacks; she had discovered the inescapable subject and object of all horror —man himself.

I felt sorry for Louise; she had a story to tell and they were disinclined to listen to her and she got on people's nerves because like the Ancient Mariner traveling the world she traveled the dayroom, stopping "one of three." One night, when I was hurrying with the herd along the corridor, I glanced in one of the side rooms and saw Louise sitting up in bed with her beautiful curly black hair cut off and her head shaved. She wore, half-on, a cotton cap. Panic seized me. I *knew*. It was happening to other people too— Mrs. Lee, Mrs. Morton, Plattie. In the morning they had been wheeled out and taken to the hospital in the city and at night they had returned with plaster over their shaven heads, and they lay in the side rooms, their faces pale and damp and the pupils of their eyes large and dark as if filled with ink. It was a newly discovered operation which was reported to "change the personality."

After her operation Louise became more docile, less inclined to fly into a rage if people refused to hear her "story"; she wet her pants and giggled delightedly, and yet began to take a pride in her appearance, but one is not sure how far that was the result of the operation or of the changed attitude towards her. She was given every attention and plied with curious morbid questions by the nurses who shuddered when they looked at her and at the others with their bald heads and said, amongst themselves, "I'm glad it's not me. It gives you the creeps."

Louise still talked of miles and miles of intestines, but it was understood that now that she had had her operation, now, it was assumed, that her personality had "changed," there was hope for her, as, conversely, there was little or no hope for the rest of us who still had our old apparently unacceptable personalities.

Louise improved. The doctor came to see her twice in one week! And then, as she stayed day after day in Lawn Lodge, and the novelty of her operation wore off, and the doctor had no more time to see her twice a week, although still docile, she grew more careless about her appearance, she did not seem to mind wetting her pants, and the nurses, feeling cheated, as people do when change refuses to adopt the dramatic forms expected of it, at the sight of the "old" Louise still settled comfortably under the "new," gave up trying to re-educate her, and very soon she was again just one of the hopping screaming people in the dayroom.

Sometimes, from my seat in the corner of the room, I saw her smile abstractedly. Miles and miles of intestines!

VII

THERE IS AN aspect of madness which is seldom mentioned in fiction because it would damage the romantic popular idea of the insane as a person whose speech appeals as immediately poetic; but it is seldom the easy Opheliana recited like the pages of a seed catalog or the outpourings of Crazy Janes who provide, in fiction, an outlet for poetic abandon. Few of the people who roamed the dayroom would have qualified as acceptable heroines, in popular taste; few were charmingly uninhibited eccentrics. The mass provoked mostly irritation hostility and impatience. Their behavior affronted, caused uneasiness; they wept and moaned; they quarreled and complained. They were a nuisance and were treated as such. It was forgotten that they too possessed a prized humanity which needed care and love, that a tiny poetic essence could be distilled from their overflowing squalid truth.

Springtime came, as far as spring happens in northern New Zealand where summer is impatient to striptease the sky and reveal brilliant days with the veils of warmth shimmering, like memory mists on the films; where winter too is importunate and will not tolerate the preceding slow melancholy of changing colors and autumn dews that are part of the southern year. The quick spring brought swelling tides of softness and warmth in the dry cold air and the smell of blossoms, the heavy honey-smell of the bush flowers, the fiery blossom of the rata tree and the fuchsia with its purple flowers like intimate folds of bruised flesh. The tuis and bell-birds returned from the deep bush and sang side by side with the migrant English thrush and blackbird; and wax-eyes, drunk with honey, teetered around by the yard fence and the fuchsia tree beyond it. Down in the yard we sniffed the air and stamped in the old puddles and watched the wet corners and the shaded places becoming dry again; and we looked over at the slate-cold sea with its scratches and patterns of depth.

The sun shone. The flies arrived, fat, and expecting to grow fatter. We had our typhoid injections. We sat on an old chair in the middle of the yard while our hair had its weekly combing with kerosene, to keep the lice at bay.

Bickerings and fist fights increased, and more people were put in seclusion; and people danced with good reason which is without reason; and the quiet people gave no sign except a twitching of their lips over their toothless gums, and their eyes stared dully from their wrinkled leaf-brown faces —the brown color that most of us had and that I had thought to be sunburn and windburn but that I realized was a stain of something else, a color of stagnancy spreading from inside and rising to the surface of the skin.

I had been allowed to keep my pink cretonne bag. I took it with me wherever I went, and it was soiled now with crumbs of old cake stuck under the cardboard base and stickings of honey on the inside. I had a copy of Shakespeare its pages thin like tissue paper and the print packed small and black and seeming wet like perpetually new footprints on the beach preserved against the obsessive shiftings of the tide. I seldom read my book yet it became more and more dilapidated physically, with pictures falling out and pages unleaving as if an unknown person were devoting time to studying it. This evidence of secret reading gave me a feeling of gratitude. It seemed as if the book understood how things were and agreed to be company for me and to breathe, even without my opening it, an overwhelming dignity of riches; but because, after all, the first passion of books is to be read, it had decided to read itself; which explained the gradual falling out of the pages. Yet at night, in the shuttered and locked room where I now slept and there was no light to read by, I would remember and say to myself, thinking of the people of Lawn Lodge, and the desperate season of their lives,

> *Poor naked wretches wheresoe'er you are*
> *That bide the pelting of this pitiless storm,*
> *How shall your houseless heads and unfed sides,*
> *Your looped and windowed raggedness defend you*
> *From seasons such as these.*

And I thought of the confusion of people, like Gloucester, being led near the cliffs,

> *Methinks the ground is even.*
> *Horrible steep . . . .*
> *Hark, do you hear the sea?*

And over and over in my mind I saw King Lear wandering on the moor and I remembered the old men at Cliffhaven sitting outside their dreary ward, and nobody at home, not in themselves or anywhere.

114

VIII

*S*AUSAGE DAY, Apple pie Day, Visiting Day, Operation Day.

Every Day.

And there was Picture Night.

At first pictures were shown on a Monday night on the wall of the stinking locked dormitory where we sat on the beds, while the patients whose beds we sat on watched jealously our forced association with the one place in the hospital that they could call their own. In this suspicious atmosphere fights usually broke out, and in the excitement beds were saturated with the odor arising almost visibly, like mists over a marsh. Eventually it was decided to show the pictures in the dayroom on the wall behind the special table.

It was summer now with long days that snapped off into a licorice dark. How could we see films in broad daylight on a cream-colored sausage-stained apple-pie-flecked plaster wall? We couldn't of course, especially as the dayroom had no blinds, but the films were shown and the frail tissue-paper images darted about upon the sausage stains and the specks of apple pie, while from the rear of the dayroom, where a timid-looking projectionist, one of the attendants, had entered cautiously carrying his flat silver box marked URGENT INFLAMMABLE and built himself a stockade of tables and forms, the whining rush of sound emerged, crackling, as if a fire were burning in the soundbox, and whooshing, like water being swept from a puddle. The jagged voices rushed out fierce and full of anger, or died with plaintive whining; sometimes shots rang out, provoking both dismay and cheers, while little Gracie ran up and shook her fist at the shadowy villain flitting about on the wall.

We saw *Scott's Last Expedition,* John Mills with his four phantom companions struggling through apple-pie-speckled snow and appearing to move, by a peculiar focal distortion, around the corner of the wall and through the dayroom door. I looked from their frostbitten hands to the infected hands and feet of the patients around me and I smelled dried urine and tasted the dirty taste that snow acquires, no matter how pure it has been when it leaves the sky, when it settles on the inhabited earth, and however deep it falls— when it becomes involved with grass and asphalt and fences and houses and prisons and aerials and church spires, and men in wildernesses. It was strange to see the men who were perhaps my first heroes, walking upon the dayroom wall, in what was meant to be "glorious technicolor," and to hear their voices over my shoulder, and remember that when I was a child I kept a red-mottled notebook where I tried to write poems, and the first one was "Captain Scott."

Captain Scott, Sand, A Longing, The Pine Trees; so that Captain Scott is mixed in my mind, not with antarctic wastes but with my own three-pine plantations, the guileless rusty sunlit first, the forbidding gloomy second which contained the den of panic, the stripling third whose trees, like young animals not allowed to grow, were always being uprooted and mutilated by the council men.

Was *Scott's Last Expedition* known to have a therapeutic effect on the mentally ill that it was shown at least three times during my stay at Treecroft and Cliffhaven? But one day, when it was announced that the evening's film would be the Marx Brothers in *A Night at the Opera*, my memories buzzed around like those pop-pop toy boats in water when you light candles in their stern. For years I had treasured the thought of that film, how we children could scarcely walk home for laughing, how arm in arm we lolled like drunks on a Saturday night along Reed Street and up Eden Street, shouting gaily as we went, "Oh that bit where he . . . that bit where she . . ." Other films—*The Ghost City* (with the sheriff being killed under the stone crusher) *The Lost Special* (with the train hurtling over the burning bridge into the alpine river and the crew and the bullion emerging unscathed in the next chapter), *The Invisible Man* (making himself invisible by pressing a button on the contraption like an old-fashioned baby-binder that he wore around his waist)—all lost their potency beside the sheer joy of *A Night At The Opera*, with the crazy flylike brothers dodging in and out of the classic scenery, being hoisted and lowered as the accessories of stage forests and chimneys, or mounted on chandeliers that tossed their sparkling horns before the outraged ample-bosomed prima donna.

I wondered who had chosen *A Night At The Opera* for screening on the stained walls of Lawn Lodge dayroom!

That night the projectionist arrived and built his fort and began at once to show the film which rushed backwards with slippery squeaks and sighs.

"I'll rewind," the projectionist said.

He rewound.

I sat self-consciously like a clerk considering the ledgers of past and present and waiting to link them by writing something in the "Carried Forward" column; the column remained almost empty. The film began, pierced with light that had the effect of rain and danced in vertical stripes and arrows across the wall. I saw Harpo with his mop of curly hair and his round sad eyes like wading pools and his harp, stolen from the weeping willow tree in Ward Seven; and the strings were broken.

And there's Groucho, slinking, cigar in mouth, into the lady's dressing room; even on the dayroom wall his eyes shine with endearing wickedness.

But the film breaks down. I have a taste in my mouth of musty cloth and I am picking at the sore on my hand that grows a scab each day like the cover of a well with myself oozing out of it.

Where's the doctor with divining twig to find if I have any self left? Where are the hooded strangers with wide black hats and staffs, to draw the sparkling blood? All things that love the sun.

> Bright shines the sun on creatures mortal,
> Men of their neighbors become sensible,
> In solitude for company.

Now Milly has made a pool on the floor and Evelyn is punching Nancy, and Piona, bored, has begun to sing at the top of her voice. Someone rushes cursing to the wall and begins to pummel it, like the knocking, in fairy stories, at the doors of secret rooms that open and are piled high with treasure. The sound garbles and complains, there is restlessness and irritation that the dim figures (with the triumph of conversion or sudden conviction) do not burst from their pallor into a decisive black and white and thereby take charge of all spheres of derangement, vacillation and confusion.

For surely the saviour will appear not in the sky or under a tree in the wilderness but over Station IZB or on the cinema screen!

And meanwhile in fits and starts the brothers caper palely up and down and arouse no laughter, not in the self-absorbed who are mad because they live so close to their own skin and its many-celled domes that are besieged with echoes from the striking moon.

We cry now.

"Right. Bed ladies. It's no use without blinds anyway."

The projectionist removes his defense of tables and is gone, and we are herded to bed and the day's thin scenery topples revealing, for those who sleep, the painted props of sleep. The rest lie in the dark and wait for morning and hope, against certain belief, that what the voices tell them is not true.

*T*HE DIRECTOR-GENERAL of Mental Hygiene," they said, "is going to visit the hospital."

Panic. He was known to be absorbed in his work (a not uncommon characteristic, it is hoped, in Directors-General) and to show a disconcerting tendency to ignore the enticing bait, specially prepared, of the observation wards and insist on sampling the conditions of the seedier "back" wards. On the day of his expected visit we were all washed, our hair was combed with kerosene to make sure there were no lice lurking, and those needing a shave were put in a queue outside the bathroom and dealt with by a nurse with a safety razor. Everybody was issued a clean smock, and as the Director was rumored to appreciate and advocate the personal touch in the nursing of the mentally ill, some patients had their hair tied with satin ribbon and a slit of lipstick etched upon their wrinkled lips. And because all of us began the day with clean clothing and all wore pants there was an unusual amount of ushering to and from the lavatories that opened off the dayroom; dingy doorless places with concrete floors, and bowls used as a favorite deposit for less orthodox treasures like torn magazines torn clothing pieces of wood, so that the bowls were usually overflowing, and men had to keep calling with rubber plungers for unblocking. On this day the lavatory was thoroughly swilled with Jeyes' Fluid.

But the flies. As it was full summer and the flies could not be warned nor would they heed the warning anyway that the Director-General was paying us a visit, some form of mass slaughter was necessary. I offered to help in this, for it meant a few minutes' escape from the dayroom, and I was learning to be cunning and to seize my opportunities, therefore I did not offer too eagerly lest I be suspected and my offer refused. I spoke casually. "I'll help—if you like."

To my delight I was given a D.D.T. spray and told to parade the corridor where the flies swarmed battening on the smell of urine and stale bedclothes and unbathed bodies.

I walked up and down spraying out clouds of D.D.T. I walked into one of the side rooms where Mrs. Holloway who had recently had a lobotomy was lying in bed; I knew she was dying. Her eyes were closed, glued by a viscous yellow crust, and her face was crawling with flies. I sprayed the D.D.T. over her face, as a necessary last rite, and left the room.

I don't know if the Director-General ever saw her; she died a few days later.

And we never saw the Director-General. What was he shown on his visit to Treecroft Mental Hospital? Did he see Ward Seven with its cheerful atmosphere, gay check tablecloths, attractive bedspreads, pastel walls, flowers?

Did they explain to him that as a contribution to the enlightened treatment of mental illness one of the young doctors had founded a dramatic club and himself performed

121

as the front half of the lion in *Androcles?* Did they tell him that dances were held and pictures shown in the big hall, attended by many of the patients from the other wards? But what of Lawn Lodge? Did he realize that food was scarce? That because we were looked upon as hopeless cases who would spend the rest of our lives in hospital we were thought not to need a share of the occasional kindness that was dispensed, on the "new" prescription, to Ward Seven and the convalescent wards?

I lost count of the months and years. I think there were one or two Christmases when a rash of stars erupted on the wall and around the door and was allowed to take its course and spread its contagion of anticipated peace for twelve days before soap and water was applied to remove it; and a bulbous multicolored paper growth swelled from the middle of the ceiling, and Matron Borough, entering the dayroom with Sister Wolf and catching sight of the swinging paper symptom, exclaimed "Ah Ah," with delight, like a physician who has traced the source of a disease, and then cried "Happy Christmas Everyone" which she meant to sound ecstatic but which, because of our past experience of her, sounded unhappily like a disguised variation of "You're for treatment."

I remember that more visitors than usual came, with yearly repentance offerings and presents such as perfume and bath oil and wave set which were collected afterwards and, still in their wrappings, stored in the suitcase room. For what use were they except as a pitiful expression of hope from those relatives who never gave up believing that some day Betty or Maggie or Minnie would shed, like an old skin, whatever had closed over their minds, and be once again just as they had been before "it" happened, before the family, recovering from the early shock and perhaps the shame of witnessing a nervous breakdown in someone they loved, had first adjusted their lives to the dictates of bus and train timetable, and long journeys to and from the hospital for visiting hours and interviews with doctors, serious men in white coats and spectacles, like in the screen advertisements for medically tested goods where germs come swarming through the air and are killed almost as if by a glance, who stared, fierce as a germ-killer, to get at family secrets. Then, as the years passed, the family responded only to the annual prodding of Christmas and the numerous Santa Clauses, red with guilt, inhabiting the greenery-festooned dens and caves of shops, to "send or take something to poor Betty." Or Maggie. Or Minnie.

Both nurses and patients were relieved when Christmas Day ended, for on that day everyone seemed beset with memories that attacked, like wasps, and were led, as memories and wasps often are, by one vindictive bully who dived in repeatedly for the kill.

But whether time was festive colored or anonymous plain it seemed curiously static, and experiencing it was like watching a spinning top and trying to believe in its scarcely visible activity and perhaps wondering whose hand held the whip that had lashed it to sleep.

I do not know, I cannot remember when it happened that the nurse came to fetch me, saying, "You're being transferred to Ward Seven," but I found myself wandering once again in the garden, with my experiences in Lawn Lodge, like the banknotes that you are told to put in small bags and attach to your underclothes when you travel in a foreign land, sewn inside my mind and being used, as one uses all past experience, as currency in my private transactions with time in its new setting, the alien brightness of Ward Seven. I was permanently afraid now and full of disbelief. There was talk of a brain operation for me, and abrupt communications like diplomatic notes between distant foreign powers passed between the doctors and my parents who then disapproved of having my brain "meddled with"! So I think I stayed all day and every day near the willow tree circling it and trying to charm it with riddles. Aunt Rose still came to see me, bringing her treat of cake and fruit and sweets; and my father journeyed up north to make the first visit he had ever made to me in hospital.

On the day of his visit I sat under the tree and hoped that I seemed calm and lucid. I knew that he would be afraid, wondering what his daughter looked like and how she behaved when she was apparently so ill that the doctors had suggested a lobotomy. I knew that Aunt Rose would be with him and her practical sorting and dispensing of the food would help, by giving the occasion the order of a ceremony, to diminish the embarrassment that my father, a taciturn man, always showed in moments of deep feeling.

Visiting time came. My father appeared alone. He sat on the seat beside me. His lip was trembling, bringing to his mouth the family pout that was selected generations ago and cosseted by heredity. He began to talk of Aunt Rose, how kind she had been to me, coming that long distance in the tram for her weekly visit.

"The fact is," my father said suddenly, "Aunt Rose is dead, Istina. She had a stroke on Thursday."

124

PART THREE

Cliffhaven

I

*A*GAINST THE DOCTOR'S wishes my sister signed me out of hospital and with her two small boys traveled south with me to my home. Her husband was to join her later for a holiday.

The family talked jokingly of my having been in the "nuthouse," and I gave them what they seemed to want— amusing descriptions of patients whose symptoms corresponded to the popular idea of the insane; and I described myself as if, by misfortune, I had been put among people who, unlike myself, were truly ill. This image that I presented of myself as a sane person caught unwillingly in the revolving doors of insanity when there was no justification for my being anywhere near the building, helped to soothe my ruffled conceit and to lessen my family's concern which was real and disturbing though it stayed beneath the surface and was revealed only in split-second gestures and expressions which nevertheless had the sustained and detailed power of slow motion.

My room at home, looking out on the holly tree and the lilac bush and the fuchsia, had a sour stale smell as if it had been prised open, like a sealed box, after many years.

My books in the bookcase and the shelves around the wall seemed to have absorbed more damp and decay in my absence, as if human contact with them had been an antidote to disintegration; little worms with black eyes had settled on the ends of the pages and begun a marathon meal that they must have thought would never be interrupted, as if the books had told them to devour devour at all costs since whoever had experienced a spiritual hunger for them had long since departed or died.

How could I help a little self-dramatization around one of the themes of living that is so consistently involved with man's mythology and religion—The Return? Although the length of time is not always relevant and there can be an acceleration of change and decay in an absence of five minutes to post a letter or fetch the groceries. I was conscious that I had been away for five years. I could not remember people and if I met them in the street and they spoke to me as if they had been friends I learned to talk to them without knowing who they were.

"Who was that?" I would say afterwards to my sister who accompanied me on these outings. And we would laugh, making fun of my memory, and we would talk together of my "country mansion" and wonder what had caused me to forget so much. In the attempted sharing of childhood reminiscences I experienced not a surge of recollected incidents and delights, but a vast invasion of loneliness. Again I could not remember, but this time, afraid to face the emptiness, I pretended memory and no one guessed.

It was autumn, with the trees in the town gardens turning gold and the mornings in chiffon mist and the cold sweat of dew clinging in chains to the grass blades. The derelict apple trees blighted and scabbed with lichen were shedding, with help from the blackbirds, their last caved-in rotten apples, and when I walked under the trees in the long damp grass, I squashed the fruit and ruined the houses of the tiny worms who had settled in for the season, webbing themselves close to the core, at the heart of the matter. All the dockseeds had ripened and fallen and the stalks of the plants were steepled with milky white "spiders' houses"; the thistledown had been blown along the high blue-and-white traffic lanes of sky; the cotton wool from the silver poplars lay in deceiving snowlike drifts under the trees.

I wandered in the paddocks and sat among the sheep. I climbed to the top of the hill where the power lines converged arterial and dark, and I listened to their humming and moaning tingle through the air. I gathered rose hips and sat beside a weather-beaten matagouri tree, reading signs in the sky, watching farmers pass in their powerful cars on their way to town or a rare leisurely gig jogging along, and sheep bleating their plaintive arpeggios, being driven up the road to the saleyards; listening to the cry of the drover as he called his dogs, and listening to the distant sound of the sea. I watched the swamp hens in their formal dress of navy blue and red sneaking with their exaggerated tiptoe motion through the swamp at the edge of the creek; and the magpies in morning suits flocking and gossiping in the gum trees, and the menacing hawks gently sliding down the wind, biding their time in the sky.

And sometimes I sat under the big rocking and sighing fir tree that was under sentence of death because it obstructed the power lines. Its boughs were laden with families of cones that the sun had long ago swelled and prised open and whose seeds were now scattered in the grass as tiny trees, already sighing in chorus at the hand of the wind. And from my seat on the hill I watched the postman cycling along the valley road, blowing his whistle as he stopped at the houses. My heart would almost miss a beat when I saw him arriving at our letter box, which was shaped like a house with a painted brick roof and painted curtains looped, according to the custom, over the front windows, and a slit in the fake front door for receiving mail. I would sneak down the hill in the shelter of the hedge, across the creek, through the pine plantations and down to the gate and the letter box. I would rush out and collect the letters and return to the safety of the pine trees.

Why?

There is no unusual explanation. I merely dreamed that a letter would come addressed to me, a love letter, that I would take it to my room and read it again and again and memorize it and pore over the handwriting and try to imitate it and change my own ink to green if the handwriting were in green ink. But who would write me a love letter?

My sister was pregnant. I cried at night in bed, with self-pity and strangeness, hiding my face in the pillow and muffling the overheard surge and sigh of the condemned fir tree, "Oh God, why am I empty?"

II

I STAYED AT HOME for six weeks. Until one night, when the phosphorescent skeletons were piled high in the paddocks for burning and grinding, and the literate wind was distributing near and far its own cultured manures, and the compulsive sea was going and coming with eternal news of itself and recent summer intimations of humanity— ice-cream cartons and orange peel—and the texture of the trees and the people in the sky seemed to have been applied like papier-mâché soaked in light, and my father groaned and my mother sat bailing the blood from her enormous shoes, I found myself in Cliffhaven, in bed in the observation dormitory and gazing with terror at the treatment room; for there was no bravery now and I could no longer pacify myself by repeating outmoded verses about apples that, free from decay and codlin moth, were lying, the fruit of dreams, in a flattery of moonlight; nor could I console myself by believing that conditions had changed, that the old threats would not be applied in order to get prompt obedience and cooperation.

"Istina's back," they said.

They looked at me with curiosity and sympathy. They

told me that Dr. Howell, "Scone," had left to take up general practice in a fashionable suburb by the sea, and any summer Sunday afternoon, said those who had contacts with the outside world, Scone and his wife and their young family could be glimpsed, with the necessary Li-Los and buckets and spades, sunning themselves on the beach. The new doctor, Dr. Steward, a tall frail-looking man in his middle thirties, seemed under the domination of Miss Glass. If he dared to take a few extra minutes to speak to a patient, Matron Glass spoke to him as if he were an erring schoolboy, and afterwards she would admonish the patient, "Why did you take up Dr. Steward's time like that? You could see he was busy. There are ninety-seven other women in this ward and not all day to attend to the likes of you."

"The likes of you," was still one of Matron's favorite phrases. Another was a sentence which began, "What she needs is—" which included Matron's special prescription of the moment and which was usually adopted by the timid Dr. Steward.

I did not stay long in the observation ward. While I was in bed Mrs. Pilling and Mrs. Everett, for old acquaintance' sake, contrived to send me small delicacies along on the dormitory tea trolley, and sometimes came to talk to me and remark, wistfully, "No one polished the corridor like you Istina." They told me excitedly that the old days of the "rubber-up" were past, that Dr. Portman was going to modernize the hospital and had begun by installing a wonderful machine, an electric polisher which also scrubbed provided you remember to turn the correct switch, but none of the patients these days had any sense of ward responsibility, nobody seemed to give the machine its proper care and it was always up in the machine shop being mended, so that the rubbers-up had to be used after all; and that just went to show, didn't it? And the daily meals were delivered to the wards now in closed vans instead of being rattled along, slopping about and gathering dust, on the backs of open lorries. And the old men didn't pull the coal carts any more, leaning and straining, two by two, like old horses between the shafts with the neat attendants walking briskly behind the cart and shouting orders; the coal was delivered by lorries with the strong young men riding on the back; and the old men stayed locked in their dayroom and fussed about, not understanding, and getting ready every morning at eight o'clock to be called to pull the carts, and some crying when no one came for them and shouted at them, "Coal! Spring to it."

Mrs. Pilling and Mrs. Everett told me who had gone home and who was still in hospital, and who had been taken to other wards; that Norma had got a job in a hostel in town and was doing fine, and that Mary had been told she could go home if anybody wanted her but nobody wanted her; that a new ward for patients like Mary and the others, an open ward, was being built up on the hill, with a wonderful view of the sea, and it was going to be the most modern ward in the hospital. But none of the patients wanted to go there, and they pleaded to be allowed to stay and sleep and eat where they had slept and eaten for twenty or thirty or forty years, and not be labeled, as the new ward was rumored to be, "Chronic." "That means we'll never get out," they said, for no matter how long they had been in hospital they still had the prerogative of secret fantastic hopes, and the labeling of them as "chronic," even when they realized they *were* chronic, seemed to exclude all hope and all the daydreams that began, "When I get out of here . . ." "Some day, when I get out in the world . . ."

In spite of the kindly hints of Mrs. Everett who worried over the polishing of the floors, I was not given the job of Chief Polisher when at last I was allowed up. Nor was my name on the important lists which hung now on the dining room wall, as part of the new "occupational" attitude. Ward Workers. Laundry Workers. Nurses' Home Workers. In the old days there had been workers, of course, but they had not been neatly listed and given a place of pride in the dining room.

I was afraid of everything. They assured me that I would not have E.S.T., but how could I believe them? How could I believe anybody? I was frightened of Matron Glass and her heavy sarcasm, her taunts, when I panicked or ran away, about "misbehavior" and "self-discipline" and her remarks that I ought to be used to life in hospital for I had been there long enough. And I was afraid of Sister Honey, of her habit of saying suddenly at breakfast time, "I'm going through your lockers today," an announcement which seemed to contain a hidden threat and which always produced a feeling of panic, as if in "going through" my locker Sister Honey would chance to find some evidence which I had forgotten or neglected to hide and which would finally incriminate me. Other patients seemed beset by the same feeling of panic, for the lockers that stood beside each bed were the sole repository of anything which belonged to us yet was vulnerably apart from us, and it almost seemed as if we left fragments of ourselves inside our lockers.

On these mornings we would hurry from the table as soon as "Rise Ladies" was said, and try by hook or by crook to reach our lockers. For those in the lower dormitories it was a simple matter; for those in the observation dormitory, where the people were locked up waiting for treatment, there were pleas to be let in only to get at our lockers and arrange things and remove evidence of secret hoarding. Otherwise dinner would be a time of reprimand and shame, with Sister Honey holding up slabs of stale crumbly cake and dirty underclothes, and reading the names; and it always seemed as if she had found out more than mere refuse, that she had, against our wishes and to our perpetual shame, penetrated our deepest secrets.

My moments of fear became more uncontrollable, and one day Matron Glass and Sister Honey gave their joint prescription, beginning, "What she needs is . . ."

"What you need," Matron said to me, "is bringing to your senses. What you need is a stay in Ward Two."

III

*S*O I WENT TO join the strange people whom I had seen before on my previous stay at Cliffhaven; and on that first day among them, when I climbed the park fence and returned to Ward Four, I was greeted with "Pull yourself together. You've been in places like that before. Don't pretend you're not used to them." And I was marched back by the Matron herself who reiterated, when handing me over to Sister Bridge. "She's used to these wards. She needs to be taught a lesson."

Part of Ward Two was a new building made to replace the old refractory ward which had been burned, with thirty-seven patients, a year before I first came to Cliffhaven. The old Brick Building was still used as the sleeping quarters, accommodating the sixty-seven women of the ward.

In Ward Two the "new" attitude was made easier to put into practice by the modern living quarters which consisted of a dining room, a "dirty" dayroom where the continually ill patients were locked and where those with intermittent attacks were kept as long as their attacks lasted; a "clean" dayroom, its walls hung with sea- and mountainscapes, its furniture new and bright (as was the furniture in the "dirty" dayroom), its wall of windows giving an occasional view of people passing and little dogs trotting and trees changing color with the seasons, so that one did not have the feeling of being immured and left to rot in an abandoned dwelling. The rest of the building consisted of a bathroom with three baths, two sets of lavatories, one doorless, the other with the doors three-quarter-length, staff office, clinic, clothing cupboard and cloakroom, and storeroom, dining room and pantry. Doors led from the ward to the yard and across the road to the park, and through the yard to the Brick Building with its locked single rooms, dirty dormitories, and upstairs open dormitories. The hospital had learned the lesson of the fire. Under Dr. Portman, sprinkler systems had been installed in all the buildings and existing fire escapes straightened and new ones built for all the upper floors.

There were no people in strait jackets in Ward Two. Cynics used to say there was no need for them as the worst patients had perished in the fire; yet the more experience one had of Ward Two the more one realized that, in any case, strait jackets were treatments, or restraining processes of the past. Whereas in Treecroft the best-cooked meals (and the most plentiful), the gayest pictures, the brightest bedspreads were to be found in Ward Seven where the so-called "sensible" patients lived, in Cliffhaven the brightest ward was Ward Two—that is, in terms of purely chromatic dispersion! And let no one imagine that the framed and glassed landscapes on the walls suffered from the attacks of the disturbed patients. Although the surroundings were not openly studied or even admired by the patients, they were not abused. Windows might be broken in the course of a day yet the pictures remained untouched and the flowers stayed in their vases. It seemed that the more articulate members of the ward exuded a fertile pride that spread and flourished silently even in the midst of what one might have called the desert of the most withdrawn patients.

Cake for tea; chocolate cake, pink-iced cake, madeira cake; and if there was not enough for all it was not, as might be supposed, the more "sensible" patients who bene-fited on the grounds of their being able to "appreciate" what they were given, but those from the dirty dayroom who had their meals in the first sitting—that is as far as any of them sat and did not stand and grab; the demented ones who spent the sunny days lying like animals shamming death in the face of great danger, or running and raging and skipping in the park or the yard. They went to bed at four o'clock in the afternoon. We used to see them rushing past the door of the clean dayroom in their dirty striped smocks, clutching their remnants of snacks—slices of rainbow sponge or fruit cake.

Sister Bridge cared for them. She told me once, in a moment of confidence which she always regretted and which caused her to show to me the kind of antagonism often felt towards those who share the secrets of our real or imagined frailties, that she had begun nursing as a timid young girl in the days when, as a matter of course, all disturbed patients wore locked boots and strait jackets; and that, after her first day on duty, she cried most of the night and resolved, though she never kept her resolution, to sub-mit her resignation and leave the appalling place and be-come a nurse in a general hospital where the patients were not shamed and abused because of their illness and where you could at least see what was wrong with them and prepare a neat dressing with ointment and clean white bandages to soothe and heal, and with no difficulty keep the patient quietly trapped in bed. But here at Cliffhaven or any mental hospital you had to provide your own bandages from within yourself to bind wounds that could not be seen or measured, and at the same time it seemed you had to forget that the patients were people, for there were so many of them and there was so much to do. The remedy was to shout and hit and herd.

Sister Bridge was now thirty-six and married to one of the attendants. Her appearance—that of a female butcher, red haired, freckle faced, fat, blowsy—was so much like that of other domineering, insensitive mental nurses that it seemed to have sought her out and attached itself to her as a camouflage in order to protect her and give her prestige among her species and safeguard her own sensitivity. She had known many of the patients for years and was loved and trusted by them and her attitude was usually one of happy sarcasm where words which came from her as sarcasm and mockery, a habit which she had perhaps acquired when learning to impress and obey the dictatorial matron of years ago, seemed in the air to undergo a transformation, to be fused with her abundance of vitality and sympathy so that they arrived without seeming to hurt. She was like a conjuror who, in mid-air, changes the fire he has breathed to wine. The patients would smile delightedly at whatever Sister Bridge said to them. Sometimes I wondered if perhaps she had not actually discarded words as a means of communication and was putting her meaning across in some other way while shouting (she usually shouted) the sort of near-abuse that one hears spoken every day by mental nurses to their patients.

Unfortunately I observed Sister Bridge too closely. This unself-conscious giving of herself to those in her care was a marvel worth watching, and it caused me great sadness when, one day, as I was standing quietly by, she noticed me and knew immediately that I had been marveling at her almost telepathic sympathy with the patients. She blushed, as if with shame, and turned angrily to me.

"Oh," she said sarcastically, "so we're observing are we? You're studying me are you, Miss Know-all? Am I doing something wrong perhaps?"

"It's not that," I said. "It's not that." And I was silent.

From then on Sister Bridge showed her resentment towards me and seized every opportunity to hurt me. By an unintentional glance I had surprised her into surprising herself into an uncomfortable consciousness that seemed to amount to fear.

Her delight now was to make me suffer and her motive was reinforced by the matron's words, "She needs to be taught a lesson."

IV

*B*UT WHO AM *I* to say that Sister Bridge was in charge of Ward Two, when the real commanders were of course Mary-Margaret and Alice? Mary-Margaret had put herself in control of the pantry, like a general occupying enemy territory. She supervised the buttering of bread, the making of toast, the cutting and distribution of cake and the washing of the containers from the big kitchen. When these were washed after each meal Mary-Margaret used to open the kitchen door and with a lusty battle cry hurl the trays down the wooden steps to lie there higgledy-piggledy until they were collected by the kitchen van. No matter how many times Sister Bridge pointed out that the trays were being damaged and that complaints were being sent from the kitchen, Mary-Margaret refused to heed. Sister Bridge would shrug her shoulders and grin and say, "Now Mary-Margaret we'll give you one more chance."

Mary-Margaret was a powerfully built straight-backed woman with snow-white hair which she usually decorated with a differently colored bandeau for each day of the week; these gave her a gypsy appearance. Her eyes, anyway, were those of a seer and one could be almost certain that whatever Mary-Margaret gazed at was something no one but herself could recognize and understand, as if, while the rest of us had studied only the primer of looking, Mary-Margaret had been a graduate for many years.

She preferred to be called Dame Mary-Margaret, and at night, when it was part of her routine to stand on the top of the stone steps in the Brick Building and give a lively broadcast to Egypt, she always signed off to the listening world as Dame Mary-Margaret. "This is Dame Mary-Margaret signing off. Goodnight Egypt. Goodnight the World. Goodnight everyone everywhere."

She would sing then,

> *Eternal Father strong to save*
> *Whose arm hath bound the restless wave,*
> *Who bidst the mighty ocean deep*
> *Its own appointed limits keep,*
> *Oh hear us when we cry to thee*
> *For those in peril on the sea.*

and conclude with a further "Goodnight the World," after which, with her many belongings which filled three bags and which she carried with her always, she would trudge upstairs to her bed in the select open dormitory.

How could Sister Bridge help treating Dame Mary-Margaret as an equal, asking her advice (since her own was so frequently ignored), and apologizing contritely when Mary-Margaret's powerful voice began to point out faults in the daily routine? Dame Mary-Margaret affirmed herself to others—as well as to herself. "This is Dame Mary-Margaret," she would shout as she opened the window to

142

throw crusts to the sparrows perched below on the kitchen trays, waiting for the forbidden tidbits.

"You're not allowed to feed the sparrows," Sister Bridge would remind her.

Dame Mary-Margaret took no notice. "God's creatures," she would call out in a military voice, and turning solemnly to Sister would address her in the formal yet dramatic tones which she usually adopted, enunciating eloquently and urgently, "Sister, we need more cake for tea," as if she were requesting supplies for those whose lives depended upon her—a stranded army or the survivors of a national disaster.

In the vicinity of Dame Mary-Margaret one had the feeling of being a human extra. She seemed to need no one and to have the power, which she did not of course exercise, of removing all superfluities like people and buildings and existing complete in her own world, which was Egypt and the deserts of North Africa.

She had one son, a handsome university student, who came to visit her. She showed no outward feeling for him but her journey to the front visiting hall was a carefully prepared campaign which ended in a victory that she shared with no one. On those days she wore two bandeaux, much make-up, including an extra layer of face powder, and returned with her three baskets laden with gifts to eat, to wear, and to keep in her locker and to gaze at suddenly in the night when the moon shone through the wire netting of the window.

Alice, who shared with Mary-Margaret the command of the domestic affairs of the ward, was also middle aged, but modest, soft spoken, dressed neatly in a striped cotton ward dress, gray stockings, and black lace-up ward shoes; with her

143

silver hair carefully covered during the day as she went about her self-imposed task of cleaning and polishing the ward. Alice seemed daily to grow thinner, and such was her serious, dedicated air as she worked that one could not believe her thinness to be the result of physical exertion but a spiritual consuming of herself. Her true place was aboard the Mayflower or in a Quaker Meeting House; or so one would have thought, until one saw her at night, in bed, combing her waist-long white hair, and by some magic process, as she shook her hair freely about her, unloosening her tight lips and talking, talking of the many times in her life when she had been kidnaped in broad daylight and smuggled aboard ships to the Spanish Main and borne away by wild men at dead of night to caves in the Himalayas. Held for ransom. Tortured. Threatened. And she spoke the truth. As she spoke, what the advertisers might call a "secret ingredient" passed her lips inside the words, and forced us to believe her stories. And then, when morning came and her hair was covered with the striped cotton cap, and she put on her ward dress, she once more assumed her prim demeanor and went discreetly and reverently about her cleaning.

The possessions dear to Alice were her polishing rags and dusters which she washed each evening and hung on the rope clothesline that stretched from outside the dirty-day-room window to the dining room window across the small gravel and grass-filled back yard. Dame Mary-Margaret and Alice were the only ones allowed outside to hang up clothes. But they ventured out cautiously, looking to left and right, and returned hurriedly as if pursued, and not until they were safely inside, behind the glass of the windows, did they regain their confidence. Alice, if she talked at all during the day, spoke of polishing, of streaks where the polish refused to be rubbed into the linoleum, of slippery places so dangerous "that anyone might break a leg"; or of Requisition Day which was Alice's personal festival when Sister Bridge invited her into the stock cupboard to choose new dusters from the discarded bed linen, and Alice would pick over the cloth, touching here, smoothing there, giving deep consideration to size and pile and durability. This process of judgment and selection was usually followed by a cup of tea with Sister Bridge and a slice of ward cake provided by Dame Mary-Margaret who, though she rarely talked to Alice, understood the importance of the occasion and liked to encourage ceremonial procedure.

Alice often told a tale which had no need of a secret ingredient to trick our disbelief, for it was true. Her breasts had been removed while she was still young. We knew that, and we turned our eyes away or gazed morbidly at her when she dragged her striped flannelette gown over her emaciated body which, though few guessed and Alice herself seemed unaware, had chosen secretly to nurse a cancer. A week before Alice died she was still working at her dusting and polishing, refusing to abandon them and in the end being forced to bed. For who, she pleaded, would wash the polishing rags? And who would know exactly which rag to use for which purpose? And who else understood the surface of the ward floor so completely, like a gardener understanding his earth, the mariner his ocean and the artist the texture of his oils?

Alice died in the night, in great pain. There was a comfort for us in knowing that the nurse on duty had a reputation for laying out the dead with care. They said she made Alice look beautiful; a touch of cotton wool here and there, her cheeks full and flushed and delicately made-up, her hands clasping fresh flowers. If one had known Alice only in the daytime as the prim hard-working maid of the ward, one would have thought that should she chance to wake and find herself wearing lipstick and rouge she would be shocked. But we had seen her in the night and heard her thrilling extravagant tales, and surely, we thought, no one would have been more pleased to spend the longest night of all transformed, though mildly, as a Jezebel.

V

*T*HE APPROACH OF night provided a signal for the release of even more screaming and shouting than had been heard during the day in the park or the yard. No sedatives were given, and from the time the people from the dirty dayroom went to bed at four o'clock, the Brick Building was a riot of noise. And always, among the others, one could distinguish Brenda's pedantic protesting voice.

I remembered Brenda from Ward Four. I remembered her as one of the first to have the "new" operation to change the personality, and how, with much talk of retraining her to adjust to what were called the ways of the world, Pavlova used to take her and the three or four other lobotomy cases, for special walks in the gardens, naming the flowers and the clouds and the incidental people and interesting her patients once more in the affairs of the world, assuming, for something must be assumed to start with, even after a lobotomy, that the affairs of the world were worthy of interest. Brenda, I learned, had been a talented girl, a pianist who was shortly to have taken a scholarship overseas. And now, five years later, she was in Ward Two, having had another operation—performed it seemed in a desperate attempt to remedy the too-soon evident and frightful effects of the first. She remembered me. I tried not to weep when I saw her condition.

When she walked she moved her hands, trying to make elaborate sculptures of the intractable air, taking careful chicken steps and at times supporting herself by sliding her hand along the wall. Forced to move from one side of a room to the other she panicked and clung to the wall until she was propelled by the scruff of her neck. Sometimes suddenly alone in the center of the room, she would overbalance and then laugh delightedly yet nervously, saying in a rush of breath, Oh dear, oh dear; and then she would turn to her brother who always followed her and whom she addressed formally as Mr. Frederick Barnes. She would curse him and add, "Get out of here, Mr. Frederick Barnes."

She called me Miss Istina Mavet. She would heave a great sigh, "Oh I envy you Miss Istina Mavet!" Then she would put her hand up the leg of her striped pants and drawing forth, after a little manipulation, a lump of feces would exclaim, "Look Miss Istina Mavet. Just look. I'm terrible aren't I? I blame Mr. Frederick Barnes for this." Her voice would deepen then and become tremendous and her face would flush purple. She would scream. Since her first operation she suffered from convulsions; often we saw her fall in a fit.

Although Brenda was more often confined in the dirty dayroom, as a special treat Sister Bridge would let her come to the clean dayroom to play the piano. She would sneak in, moving her hand along the wall, and approach the piano and, after lifting the lid of the stool the correct number of times in accord with her secret personal rhythm, she would sit down, shrugging her shoulders with pleasure, and begin to giggle in a deprecating way, blushing and staring at the piano as if it had begun to pay her compliments. It shone ebony; she could see her face in it, even the shadowy hint of her dark mustache. She would continue to giggle, clasping and unclasping her hands and adopting now postures of delight as if the piano were communicating good news to her; and then, in a flash, she would remember Mr. Frederick Barnes.

"Get out of here, Mr. Frederick Barnes," she would rage, dropping her hands quickly to her lap as if she had been putting them to immodest use without knowing that she had been observed. "Get out, Mr. Frederick Barnes."

And turning to the patients who were now interested and waiting for her to play, for we liked her playing, she would excuse herself. "It's Mr. Frederick Barnes. I hate him. I hate him. Ho Ho, Mr. Frederick Barnes. And I, of course, am Miss Brenda Barnes of Cliffhaven Mental Hospital."

Then she would smile wistfully and break into a giggle and begin to play, gently and carefully, a few bars of what the patients called "classical."

Carol would interrupt. "That's classical. Play *Moonlight Sonata*."

Carol, a dwarf, and Big Betty, over six feet tall, were in self-appointed command of the clean dayroom.

So Brenda tempered the music to the demands of pale freckle-faced Carol who, in talking of her own origins used to say, "I'm jitimate. My mother had me before she married. She didn't want me to grow."

"Play Butterfly Grieg Brenda. Play *I'm Always Chasing Rainbows*."

(*I'm Always Chasing Rainbows* was a Chopin melody made popular when Cornel Wilde as Chopin, in the film *A Song to Remember*, found time between gazing tenderly into Mlle. Dupin's eyes, to flick his fingers over the piano keys and be ghosted into playing brief catchy versions of his own alleged compositions.)

At first Brenda played lovingly, remembering every note, although her sense of time seemed to have suffered. She played on and on after a while ignoring Carol's pleas "not to play classical." Listening to her, one experienced a deep uneasiness as of having avoided an urgent responsibility, like someone who, walking at night along the banks of a stream, catches a glimpse in the water of a white face or a moving limb and turns quickly away, refusing to help or to search for help. We all see the faces in the water. We smother our memory of them, even our belief in their reality, and become calm people of the world; or we can neither forget nor help them. Sometimes by a trick of circumstances or dream or a hostile neighborhood of light we see our own face.

In the midst of her playing Brenda would suddenly stop, clearly struck by the irrevocability of her situation, and begin to rage and scream and thump violently and abusively upon the keys, banishing the music which retreated like an animal that, awakened from hibernation by the warmth and light of a false spring, is forsaken by the sun and faced with the continuing desolation of winter.

A restlessness would invade the dayroom. One or two patients would wander up to the piano and tinker with the treble notes or plong the bass and shout to Brenda to go to hell.

Carol would take comand again. "We've had enough of

you, Brenda. We want the radio on anyway. Let Minnie Cleave play something."

In disgrace Brenda would be led back to the dirty dayroom while Sister Bridge could be heard threatening, "Never again, Brenda. It always ends up like this with your shouting and rampaging."

So we sat around in the clean dayroom, frustrated and uneasy. The spectacle of Brenda at the piano gave the feeling that one had witnessed the kind of earth tremor that in two instants uncovers and reburies the lost kingdom.

But, "Minnie Cleave play for us," Carol would be shouting, and Minnie would look up from her handkerchief which she studied like a plan all day. "No no," she quavered, at the same time deciding that she would enjoy playing, and then her small bowed figure, bag in hand, would creep up to the piano, and Minnie, a former Mother Superior in a convent, would tinkle monotonously over and over until she was forced to stop,

> *The Campbells are coming, hurrah, hurrah,*
> *The Campbells are coming, hurrah.*

VI

*S*INCE THE DAY when I observed Sister Bridge and unintentionally surprised her into self-consciousness, she had been antagonistic towards me, almost afraid of me. Sometimes it seemed as if we shared a dreadful secret; sometimes I had the fantastic idea that we were two hawks in the sky, as distant from each other as opposing winds, who had both swooped at a precise moment upon the same corpse and, on beginning to scavenge it, had found it to be composed of decaying parts of our two selves. Had I mentioned this fantasy to Sister Bridge she would have sneered; she sprayed all fantasy with contempt in order to hide from it and escape its danger and try thus to control the sinister movement of it. She emitted scorn as an octopus in a similar situation emits clouds of ink.

I tried to understand her attitude towards me. When I was overcome by panic and ran from the meal table she ordered the nurse to drag me by the hair and accused me of "creating a fuss to get attention."

"There's nothing to be afraid of. Think of other people for a change, Miss Know-all."

And was I not thinking of other people? Did not the

thought of the tragedy of the people around me, particularly of Brenda and her worsening condition, make me whisper into the dark at night when I lay in the small room, the comforting platitude for use in disaster, in shipwreck air raid flood and bomb cloud, God help us Oh God help us? And I remember that I prayed the charm prayer which I had somehow felt compelled to say to myself every night of my life since I learned it at school and was given a small brass medal the size of a halfpenny with the prayer printed on it. It was more a feat of printing than a religious token and I marveled at it the way one marvels at ships in bottles or the contents of the Encyclopaedia Britannica reproduced on a scroll of magnetic tape. Yet I had felt bound to repeat the prayer and to follow it with a blessing for everyone in the family and the hope that I would be a "good girl." I used to want to bless myself too but I felt it would not be allowed; it was rather more serious than sharing out sweets and self-righteously keeping one's choice to the last, in spite of the desire to grab. So I was content with asking that I be a "good girl." And now what did Sister Bridge and Matron Glass mean when they asked that I "think of others for a change?" It occurred to me, frighteningly, that Matron and Sister Bridge had known me all my life and had spied on me even when I was a child.

They must have seen me steal money, and pinch the baby on its arm, and sneak the doctor's book from the top of the wardrobe. And had they listened to my prayers and noted that I prayed only for my family and myself and did not think to bless the people next door who always lent us the evening paper before they read it themselves, or the poorer children with their fathers on the dole, or the boy with his leg in a brace, or the little girl who stank and was never asked to join the game where Poor Sally sits weeping for a playmate and is invited to choose one from all the clean fresh-dressed little girls bobbing around?

After breakfast (a bowl of porridge, bread and butter or toast, tea) which was taken in one sitting, the nurse called, "Lavatory, Ladies," and everyone queued to sit in the doorless cabinets under the supervision of a nurse. At the beginning of my stay in the ward I refused to go to the lavatory while I was being watched, but the nurse pulled down my pants and forced me onto the seat, at Sister Bridge's command. "You need the discipline of a ward like this," was Sister Bridge's constant remark. After we had been to the lavatory a nurse called, "Dirty Dayroom" or "Yard" or "Park" and those going there would be shepherded out while the rest of us waited for the order, "Brick, Ladies," whereupon we trooped over to the Brick Building to repair the damages of the previous night by changing and making the beds, scrubbing and polishing the floor, and shining the brass handles that were fixed to the outside only of the single rooms.

My task was the "back" corridor and its single rooms. Dirty mattresses had to be carried out, emptied, the cover put in the laundry basket, and clean covers filled with fresh straw from the mattress shed. The wet mattress covers were left near the pipes in the shed to dry. Sometimes I would sneak out and hide in the warm mattress shed with its stuffy sour smell of evaporating urine and human manure and stable straw, and I would see one of the nurses there who had wanted a "quiet smoke" and she would talk to me in spite of the orders given by Sister Bridge that no members of the staff were to talk to me.

"Why does she hate you so much?" they asked. "Why is she so afraid of you? What have you done?"

After work we returned to the dayroom where we spent the time in a sporadic kind of occupational therapy interspersed with crazy cross-conversations, nipped quarrels and futile musings. We were glad when dinnertime came and we saw the people from the park being hurried over the road and into the dining room for the first sitting. Only once or twice during my three years' stay was I put in the dirty dayroom and made to go to first sittings of meals. Why, there was almost a shipboard snobbery about eating, except that there was no controversy about who should or should not sit at the Captain's table!

The only survivor from the old refractory-ward fire was Big Betty who was rumored to have started the fire herself, perhaps intentionally, with a cigarette butt. This accusation returned from her remote conscience like a radar signal bounced from the moon. Big Betty was grandiose and uncompromising. She was over six feet tall, and bore with her everywhere her two bags of treasure which included old magazines and two or three pairs of worn-out slippers. She refused to work at the Brick and her refusal was accepted. She preferred to stay in the clean dayroom, lying on her special sofa like Madame Recamier, her big feet stuck in the air like frog-men flippers. Her voice, not wishing to be outdone by her size, emerged as a roar.

"Istina!" she used to bellow suddenly so that I leapt with fright.

"Now a young girl like you, now someone like you,

I can understand someone like me, but someone like you
. . ." she would reflect a moment, rubbing her large purple
nose, and then roar, "What are you doing in this ward?"
As if I had been accused of a grave crime I would try to find
an excuse to offer the prosecuting Big Betty, but she had
forgotten her own question and would boom, "Istina, go
and see to that poor soul over there!"

I would go and see to the "poor soul"—it was Minnie
Cleave who kept losing her handkerchief among the things
in her little cloth bag, and she would get in such a panic
if she could not find it, whimpering and moaning and turning everything on to the floor, and then kneeling and beginning to pray. She had transferred the meaning of her
life to her handkerchief, as a child, after a long confusing
day at the beach, takes home safe in her handkerchief her
treasure of a few shells and bright stones, the meaning of
her day.

Whatever was captured within her handkerchief was no
comfort to Minnie. She was nearly always depressed. Sometimes they gave her E.S.T. and she returned pale and dazed
and wanting her bag and her teeth and not being able to
remember where she had hidden them. Big Betty would
know. Big Betty saw everything. She looked upon Minnie
with the sympathetic contempt that the invincible may
show to those who succumb.

I was afraid of Big Betty.

"Istina," she would thunder, "when are you getting out
of here? Answer me!"

I would murmur something in a scared voice and then
Edith, who was Mrs. Everett's sister-in-law and who always
referred to herself in the third person, would come up

to me and take my hand and, trying to look fierce but succeeding only in looking comical, for she was a timid slight person, would address Big Betty in a piping voice, "Now don't you go frightening her. Now Edith will look after you, Istina. Now don't be afraid. You know Edith, Mrs. Everett's sister-in-law that drowned her little girl, drowned her little girl she did."

"Aw shut up Edith Everett," Carol would cry out, "let's hear the radio, *Walking My Baby Back Home!*"

Carol controlled the radio. She had been in hospital since she was twelve and she was now twenty-one, with the body of a child of ten and a pale aged face with dark rings beneath her eyes. She talked constantly of "getting out of this dump" and of marrying, and she exchanged loving notes through the window with the tow-haired pig-boy. She worked hardest of all in the Brick Building and was like a little dog always at Sister Bridge's heels, wanting to do things for her and run messages and carry baskets, especially the empty canteen basket.

Under the Social Security administration every patient was given four shillings a week pocket money. For those whose condition prevented them from spending their own money Sister Bridge bought cakes and sweets and made sure they were distributed fairly with none of the degrading "lolly scrambles" that were the Lawn Lodge routine. All who were well enough to make the journey to the canteen looked forward with mounting excitement to Friday afternoon. Four shillings! What would we buy? Few of the patients had visitors, and I seldom had a visitor, therefore part of my four shillings was spent on food. We could buy toothpaste, soap for those who wanted a change from the ward soap, sweets and biscuits and make-up, lipstick and powder, and novelties like paper flowers that unfold and bloom in water and necklaces and rings . . .

At two o'clock on Friday afternoon Sister Bridge appeared in the doorway of the dayroom with the empty laundry basket, and Carol rushed forward to help her.

"Right!" Sister Bridge would exclaim. "Canteen, Ladies!"

So we straggled along past the Watch and the Laundry and the Big Kitchen and the cobbler's where the elderly patient with long brown hair falling about his shoulders sat repairing the ward shoes, and the carpenter's with its whirring machines and its floor littered with shavings, to the Canteen. The dazzle and wonder of the stacked goods inspired us with awe which was natural when one remembers that many of the patients had not been inside a real shop for twenty or thirty or more years, and the hospital canteen was the nearest they would get now, in their lifetime, to the excitements of flamboyant commerce, the tensely boxed and parceled shapes and sizes of various gloss and glitter.

Sometimes the canteen proprietor who was assisted by a patient (with an impractical and admirable habit of giving over-full measure when weighing the sweets) would seem to show nostalgia for the ways of shops "in the world," and would have a "special line" displayed on the front of the counter—a cheap ballpoint pen, a sparkling bangle or necklace, a badge to wear at cocktail parties, a clip-on tie for the men to wear with evening dress; and Sister Bridge, after collecting the ward requirements would be standing at the back of the room watching, trying to curb the ecstasies of those patients who found it hard to resist a seductive but apparently useless bargain.

"Remember you'll have no money left for anything else."

The dazzle made my heart beat fast and my head swim, and all thought of what I had planned to buy vanished from my head, and on being urged forward by Sister Bridge I would hold back, saying, "I'll wait a while and think," to which the retort would be, "So we have all day so you can choose, have we? Let me tell you young lady I'm getting back in time for my cup of tea."

One day Carol, who had been talking more than usual about marriage, bought a scintillating stone ring which she proclaimed to be "real zephyr" and which she slipped carefully on to what she called her "gagement finger."

"I'm gaged now," she announced. "I'll soon be married."

No one contradicted her. When you have been in hospital long enough you tend to lose the urgent need, taken for granted in the "outside world," to express disbelief; it seems pointless, even a presumption, to burst out with cries of "That's not true" when you realize that truth is the indestructible foundation of the foundation of the foundation and needs no defense anyway.

Carol's ring cost three and sixpence, and with her remaining sixpence she bought conversation lollies in the shape of pastel-tinted and perfumed hearts with exclamatory endearments printed on them which Carol asked Hilary to read for her as Carol had never learned to read or write and needed help even with her love letters to the pig-boy. The hearts said I Love You, Love Me, Sweetheart, Crazy You, Tip-Top and Let's Get Married, the letters in the last one being rather small and cramped in order to fit on the heart. No one could subdue Carol on that day, for she was visited by three successive delights, and had she been able to write poetry she might have celebrated them in the tradition of

> A *rainbow and a cuckoo's song*
> *May never come together again,*
> *May never come*
> *This side the tomb.*

First was the "gagement ring" with its "genuine zephyr" which meant that she was "practically married"; next the bag of conversation lollies to pass through the window to the pig-boy, and perhaps to keep for somebody "handsome" at the fortnightly dance in the hall. And lastly, that same evening, over the radio, came Carol's favorite song which she sang in her tuneless voice, remembering a few words here and there,

"Some enchanted evening, you may see a stranger . . ."

At the Canteen I bought myself sweets which I did not like to eat by myself and which I offered to the other patients. I was reprimanded by Big Betty, "Istina, eat them yourself."

Sweets, and a writing pad and new pencil, and I would sit down determined to write a letter.

Ward Two, Cliffhaven Mental Hospital, I would head the page; and then overcome by the futility of saying anything to anyone and having no one to say it to, I would close my pad and put it in the imitation-leather bag where I kept my treasures—the Shakespeare growing daily shabbier with non-reading, the *Sonnets To Orpheus* in German and English.

"*Wolle die Wandlung*," I read. "Choose to be Changed."

Not only Rilke was giving that advice. The doctors were to have consultations, and Sister Bridge was hinting to me that it was impossible for me to continue living as myself, that I must be changed.

That which would stay what it is renounces existence;
Does it feel safe in its shelter of lusterless gray?

they might have whispered to me, but for them there was one way only, the head shaved and the eyes large and dark, meeting darkness.

"Choose to be changed; with the flame with the flame be enraptured"—but in too many cases the flame was the ice pick of a lobotomy.

VII

*E*VERY MONTH A group of women whom we called "The Ladies" arrived from an Institute in the city to visit us. They were mostly middle aged with felt hats stout shoes and large handbags uniformly brown and shut with scrolls of dim brass that demanded a strong switch of the hand, like the turning on of a tap, to open. The ladies smelled like retired schoolteachers, with a mixture of loss and love and arrowed diagrams and small print with asterisks to indicate the foot of the page where some-one has erased the reference. They were timid and kept in a flock as they toured the dayroom, and before they ad-dressed each patient they looked about them with a furtive embarrassed air. They were not sure how to talk to us or what to say; they had learned somewhere that a fixed smile was necessary, therefore they smiled.

We felt our power over them and some of us uncharitably despised them, for they did not seem to be able to make up their minds whether we were deaf or dumb or mentally defective or all three, so that when they spoke they raised their voices and moved their lips with exaggerated care, and their vocabulary was the simplest, in case we did not understand. Sometimes they gesticulated as if we were foreigners and they were the visitors to our land who needed to try and talk our language. They wanted so much to feel at home with us, to be accepted among us, to sit and chat with us in a friendly cozy manner. They were pathetically eager to be surrounded with smiles and cheerful cries of welcome. It was not difficult to imagine "The Ladies" themselves clinging to their bags, sitting all day in the hospital sewing room or wandering in the park or yard; sometimes it seemed that they came to visit us because they had a secret affinity with us.

"Hello," they would exclaim with a heartiness that did not conceal their apprehension. "Would you like a sweetie?" And they would produce a bag of sweets, offering trustfully the whole open bag and looking shocked, tutting and finally quivering with the necessary smile, when sometimes the whole bag was snatched from them.

One of the few rewards of their visit came to them when they approached Carol. The rest of us, though we delved for the offered sweets, were suspicious and hostile, particularly as "The Ladies" said the wrong thing too many times and asked too many questions which did not bear answering and tried to cheer up people who had been in hospital twenty or thirty years by saying, "Never mind, you'll soon be home won't you?" Carol talked to them without reserve or suspicion, recounting the activities of the ward, and confiding freely her own longings, how she would soon be getting married and "getting to hell out of this dump." She showed them her "gagement ring."

"It's a zephyr," she said proudly. "Everyone with a gagement ring gets married."

"The Ladies" reacted to Carol as a zoologist might when meeting for the first time a species that conforms to all the generalizations made about it. Carol was the perfect "mental patient." For years now the same "Ladies" had been making the tiresome journey in the slow smoky train north to Cliffhaven, and returning from their visit with irritating memories of having tried to humor people who didn't need humoring, and to cheer those who couldn't be cheered. Anxiously, effusively, "The Ladies" talked to Carol and humored her and cheered her.

"Yes, I'd like to come to your wedding." "It's a lovely ring, Carol." "Of course you'll be out of here long before your wedding." Then, their cheeks flushed, their eyes bright with the success (and the strain) of their visit, they would move quickly towards the dayroom door, calling grateful good-byes to Carol and making the general promise to us all that if we were good and settled down they would come again next month with more sweets. Their faces would show just a hint of panic as they waited for the nurse to let them out, for it is unpleasant to be locked in and not have your own key, and strange things happen sometimes to visitors in mental hospitals, inexplicable things that never get into the papers!

A more sophisticated visitor who also came every month to see us was the man from the Patients' and Prisoners' Aid Society whom we called the "One-Lolly Man" because, understanding our impetuosity and greed, when he produced his paper lollies he never offered the whole bag but carefully extracted one, holding it up by its paper tail like an angler's catch and asking quietly and with a "frank" attitude that almost made one think he was going to talk about sex, "Would you like a lolly?"

Although we laughed at him for his parsimonious and cunning ways we always accepted his offering. He was a tall thin tired-looking man carrying a worn briefcase; he looked like a meter reader or an income-tax investigator or an apologetic debt collector, and we never knew what he carried in his briefcase, for he kept the bags of lollies in the pockets of his suit. He displayed none of the heart-to-heart gush of "The Ladies"; he did not ask us questions or try to engage in conversation. Except for his offering of the lollies he scarcely seemed to be aware of our presence and emptied the bags as a sort of lonely ritual in which he and the lollies were the main concerns and we, the patients, were but incidental. There was a secrecy in his giving; he was like those people who drove miles under cover of darkness to unload secret personal litter in the lonely waste places. He was grave and absorbed.

And always (to our regret) he was strictly a One-Lolly Man. Rumor said that he paid from his own pocket for sweets for the entire hospital. He toured the prisons as well. But while I was still in hospital he retired from the Patients' and Prisoners' Aid Society and went to live up north on the east coast where the palm trees grow, and he took with him the forty-nine-piece dinner set they had presented to him. And his briefcase? And a bag of paper lollies to eat on the train?

And every Christmas, instead of every month, the new Secretary came to visit us to carry on the one-lolly tradition. His sweets were gaudier, fatter, richer; but he was not a man with a dream inside him.

VIII

*W*ARD TWO WAS raised several feet above
ground level on wood and stone stilts like a boathouse
which must be kept beyond reach of the tide; I was ever
conscious of a wavelike motion of the floor which made
the building seem more like a boat that had slipped its
moorings and was adrift in the open sea. On the day that
I really believed what they had been telling me for the
past few years now—that I would be in hospital for the
rest of my life, the floor of the dayroom seemed to change
to layers of shifting jagged slate that cut into my feet, even
through the thick gray ward socks which were soon saturated
with blood seeping through upon the slates and flowing
swiftly through the door, with cut-out silver and gold stars,
for good conduct, floating upon it. I found it hard to walk
upon the sharp slates; peering through the clefts I noticed
that the building was still secure on its wooden and stone
foundations that were crusted with barnacles and wound
with strands of rust-colored rubbery sea plants; the sea
gushed and slapped and the reek of salt was carried through
the slates into the dayroom.

No one noticed. I was confounded, but no one noticed.
The sharks have a nose for blood, I thought. And soon the

lifeguards bearing their golden banner will march this way and rescue me. Will they?

The turbulent starlings dance now over Rabbit Island; the trinket light is displayed behind glass at a price that I cannot afford.

And I wanted to be alone; away from the noisy screaming people and the sad spectacle of their behavior and of their diminishing and finally vanished identities. In the end those in the dirty dayroom were mere nicknames, like the people of Lawn Lodge. There was Tilly who lived and moved in a perpetually crouching position, who never spoke but ate voraciously, her eyes glittering with a secret fire, her nose drooped to meet her chin giving her a witchlike appearance. Where was the former Tilly, the wife and mother of three children? How can people vanish without a trace and still be in the flesh before you? And it startled one to be told that Lorna had been a cultured intelligent woman. What now immovable debris of sickness had fallen from the sky to blanket an ordinary human landscape and give it this everlasting winter season? What cruel snowfall that would not melt and let ideas bud and feelings build with the far-gathered sticks and straw of human contact? And where were the snowplows trying to clear a path to the buried landscapes?

You free corny cliché sun, the red-flannel warmer of frozen places and buds in bed, I know there is a scramble for a share of you, but come down through the snow at last.

Sometimes one would surprise a human look on the face of Tilly or Lorna or the others but there was no way to capture it; one felt like an angler who discerns the ripple of a rainbow fish which will surely die if it stays in the foul water. How to trap it without hurting it? But the ripple of humanity may take the forms of protest, depression, exhilaration, violence; it is easier to stun the beautiful fish with a dose of electricity than to handle it with care and transfer it to a pool where it will thrive. And it may take many hours and years angling for human identity, sitting in one's safe boat in the middle of the stagnant pool and trying not to panic when the longed-for ripple almost overturns the boat.

I ran away.

The sun was shining, filtering warmly through the high cloud that swelled and separated, layer by layer, like cotton wool on the blue oven shelves, and I was lying on the grass in the park, staring up at the sky and blocking my ears to the screams around me and my eyes to the weather-stained and animal-stained people. There was plenty of room in the park. The patients walked or ran round and round inside the high fence where they had worn a track, a hospital stadium; or they lay, as I did now, quite still on the burned grass. From the top of the sloping park you could look down on the sea: the wind blew fresh and clear. I think it was a spring day.

I rely so much on the sun; I think of the sunflowers with their ebony hearts and their searing ragged corona and their heads turned to the sun. I think it is the removal of the sun's influence that has made us mad; the sun is blocked that used years ago to scrape the unreal shadow from our brain. So I always make a field, and I plant sunflowers, and their shadows move gently in the snow, and I pick up the pieces of dull stones that once were thoughts in precipitate flight in a friction of fire, like shooting stars in the sky.

I lay in the park and I touched the short stalks of rye and couch grass and watched the beetles twisting in and out of the burned forest, and the unsuspecting ladybirds that would have to be told of their house on fire and their children all alone; and the blind blue and pink worms emerging moist from the deep earth. In the corner near me Totty was rocking happily up and down, her hand pressed between her thighs; then she began to scream at the top of her voice, "Stop it Totty, Totty, Totty," and a shuddering groan broke from her and she withdrew her hand, covered with blood, for she was menstruating and could not be made to wear a napkin; or pants or shoes; and sometimes she tore off her clothes. Totty was fifteen.

I had no place to go to be rid of the unhappiness around me. Sometimes, in my mind, I dressed the people in ordinary clothes, rubbed the dreadful stain of hospital from their skin and put teeth in their mouths, put make-up on their faces, gave them handbags to carry and gloves to wear, and then I thought in my naïve way that I had transformed them into ordinary people, people you meet in the street and talk to and for whom you feel only the fleeting despair that is aroused by all attempts at human communication. But I could not presume to change the thoughts and feelings of my fellow-patients when they were known only to themselves. What was inside their minds? Although I might have dreamed of removing their stained skin and of putting teeth in thir toothless gums, in the end perhaps what I might have put in the place of their secret thoughts and feelings, the so-called "ordinary normal" thoughts, would have been of less value to the sum of truth than the solitary self-contained worlds they had created for themselves. Their minds were planets in their private sky and their behavior gave little evidence of their real night and day and the pull of their secret tides; their heavenly collisions storms floods droughts and seasons of strength.

The clouds raced high now in the warm spring wind. I took off my cardigan and crept to the part of the fence that was hidden by the shelter shed—a dilapidated place with khaki mounds in the corners where the people had run to mess, like dogs; then I hauled myself to the top of the fence, climbed quickly over, and dropped, with my heart beating so fast that I could scarcely breathe, into the bushes that were grown outside the park to hide the rubbish—shoes crusts excrement rags, and to secure the sad sight within from the prying eyes of wandering strangers visitors or people from the convalescent ward who sometimes felt a desire to see "what the patients in the park look like."

I know. I had experienced the morbid curiosity. I once looked through at the men prowling unshaven in their tattered outlaw clothes, and I could not forget their hopelessness; it seemed deeper than that of the women, for all the masculine power and pride were lost and some of the men were weeping and in our civilization it seems that only a final terrible grief can reduce a man to tears.

I came from the bushes and began to walk slowly along the road outside the ranch where the attendants lived, on and on past the big kitchen and the mortuary and the watch and the canteen. I was trembling and almost crying. I met Eric, my constant partner at dances, and greeted him with, "It's a lovely day. I'm lucky to have parole."

I hoped that he would not notice my slippers for he was a trusted patient who believed with the others that I was in hospital for my "own good," and he would report me if he became suspicious.

The air was yellow with catkin dust and sweet with the smell of hawthorn as I walked out of the hospital grounds, down the roads past the front gate and the cattle stop and the doctor's house. I could afford to breathe now, and walked slowly past the village school with its playground of cracked and bubbled asphalt and sprays of bright green weeds that the big boys chipped with the school hoe on Friday afternoons. A little boy was wandering from the main building towards the lavatories, stopping to scuff and stamp and investigate the familiar, making the most of the exciting solitary journey that is the loot of the ancient blackmail, "Please Sir, may I leave the room?" Others were in the classrom singing "Come O Maidens" and "Like to the Tide Moaning in Grief by the Shore," an elegy that on a spring day summoned a rush of nostalgia for the wild bush and beach and the pristine silence. I walked on and on. I arrived at the railway station. Where could I go? I approached the stationmaster, "May I use your phone, please?"

He glanced at me curiously. "Certainly."

I rang Ward Two at the hospital and asked for Sister Bridge, and she gave a gasp of amazement when I said "This is Istina Mavet here." Had I escaped only to announce myself to Sister Bridge in the hope that from a distance, without seeing me and thus not having the urge to peek at me as at a sick hen, she would realize that I did not need to be taught this everlasting "lesson" which she conspired with Matron Glass to teach me, that I did not need to be "changed" by operations on my brain, that I had never been born with an enclosed leaflet in which the "management undertakes to replace or renew all goods not found satisfactory?"

"This is Istina Mavet," I repeated over the phone, defiantly.

And then I was afraid, for they would come and get me and perhaps I would be punished with seclusion.

"Where are you speaking from?"

"You won't put me in a single room if you get me?"

"I don't make bargains. Where are you speaking from?"

I told her. She hung up impatiently and almost before I had put down the receiver a black government car carrying Sister Bridge arrived outside the station. She got out, telling the driver to return to the hospital, that she would walk with me, "and no funny business, my lady."

"Come on rag bag," she urged.

"You won't lock me up in a room?"

"I don't make bargains."

I walked with her. She looked uncomfortable with the warmth of the day and the rush of having to get down to the station, and her cheeks were blotched red, and bubbles of sweat showed where the neck of her uniform fastened in front. Just below, her unwieldy breasts bulged like pumpkins in a string bag. Her neck, like skin-colored sand, was streaked with the tide of red. I felt her beside me; I felt her discomfort in the heat. And I hated her, I hated her, but I wanted to pummel her mounds of flesh the way

I had seen the man pummeling the blubbery stew in the kitchen at Treecroft and I wanted her to speak, for her voice to be drained of the sarcasm and bitterness and self-consciousness and fear that it held whenever she addressed me.

Who was she? Was she my mother? I wanted to hit her and to climb crying on to her lap and plead to be forgiven. We walked in silence. She stopped at the village store and I followed her into the dusty room with its conglomerated display of mops buckets soap and food, and the man behind the counter, knowing Sister Bridge, and guessing that I was a patient, put on the special look which people acquire when they are faced with the "mentally ill"; a guarded fearful expression which they try to hide with overcheerfulness.

"Hello, hello, hello," he triplicated, beaming.

Sister Bridge, in a leisurely akimbo off-duty voice that I rarely heard, asked for two ice creams, handed me one, collected her change, and motioned me out of the shop.

We set out once more, licking our ice creams, towards the hospital.

"You needn't think," she warned, "that because I bought you an ice cream you won't get punished."

"You won't lock me in a room?"

"We'll see."

Suddenly she waved her arm in the direction of a small house, standing with its back to the railway cutting, in a weedy wilderness of garden.

"That's were I live," she said in a flat voice.

"And is that your car?"

"Yes, that's our car. Can you drive?"

"No. I could never learn."

"You want to learn to drive. At first I was terrified, I really was terrified—you needn't think you won't be punished, my lady."

"You won't lock me in a room?"

"We'll see. And what is there about my house that you have to stare at it?"

The house made me feel lonely. It reminded me of the first house I ever lived in, in a wilderness of a one-street town, with water drawn from the pump, and an outhouse which, although it had black beetles and wood lice, did not threaten at the base of a porcelain glacier to sweep one away with the tide every time the chain was pulled—no, a comfortable outhouse with the mess accumulating and being taken away by the night man; and no startling immediacy of electric light blazing from the center of the ceiling, but kerosene lamps with dirty wicks burning and molding soft blue shadows.

And I sat all my life in a gasoline shed under the walnut tree in Sister Bridge's house, with the cow Beauty breathing in my face her yellow and green breath of chewed grass. Her teeth were worn, like square white stools often sat upon; a drop of water, like a tear, ran from the corner of her eye down her golden face. Sometimes her behind opened like a crinkled mouth and golden skitter squirted out; and sometimes a streak of foamy pee splashed from the slit by her behind, and blood dripped out, tangling with slimy stuff around her tail. And when I lived in that little house my mother lived there with me, taking out her floppy titties to feed the baby and sometimes giving me a taste, or squeezing a jet of Beauty's milk into my mouth. So which was Beauty and which was my mother and which was Sister Bridge? And what about my father going backwards and forwards in a peaked cap with a silver badge?

Sister Bridge was my mother. I licked at the softening ice cream and walked with her up the country road with its overhanging sweet hooks of hawthorn, over the cattle stop, around the corner to Ward Two, and then I realized that I had been cheated into returning to the place which I had cried to leave. It was a trick.

Once inside Sister Bridge said to me in her usual sarcastic voice, "Get into the dayroom, rag bag, and don't try anything with me. A person of your education ought to be ashamed of herself."

She spoke fiercely and my heart sank; but she did not lock me in a room and she did not speak to me again as if she were a human being; not for a long time; and she was ashamed of having bought me an ice cream and having pointed out the place where she lived.

She had no children; not unless you count Dora Brenda Carol Totty Mary-Margaret and the many others who responded less to their names than to pulling and pushing by the neck of their faded smocks.

So I hurt her.

She went ahead of me down the stairs into the yard and suddenly I pushed her in the back and she fell, with a cry of anger and pain. I had pummeled her at last, her fat corseted body set on top of the lumpy legs that the white stockings gave a shine to, on the shins. Her big feet bulged from the duty shoes peeling white where the shoe polish pasted itself away in layers. I had pushed her and

175

I wanted to run to her and put my arms around her because she was my mother and I had caused her pain.

"You little bitch. You did that deliberately."

I went white and began to cry. I knew that she would never forgive me, that our contract of enmity was signed and sealed, surprisingly enough, with my love which I had shown by rushing at her and thumping her soft belly, knocking, like a demand to be let in out of the dark, to seek shelter from the special storm cloud which hung over me dispensing a significance of private rain.

Let me in!

"I am sorry," I said, as if reluctantly. "I didn't mean it."

"You bitch. You cunning bitch!"

*N*OW HILARY. She was infatuated with Harry although she could not quite forget Peter whose child she had while she was married to Geoffrey.

Hilary was one of the few patients who could talk "sensibly," and, like Carol who could also talk "sensibly," her conversation was mostly about men; Carol talking about the man she was "gaged to" and Hilary about the men she had loved. Hilary was in her early thirties with fine golden hair which she described as "baby-soft," thin lips with tiny biting spots on them, plump hands like soft shapes of wax, and smooth pale legs crossed at a studied angle beneath her tight black skirt whenever Dr. Steward entered the room. She was prepared for every man, even Dr. Steward, to make love to her. She had one child by her husband Geoffrey and one by her lover Peter and planned to have one by Harry, the male patient who now occupied most of her thoughts which emerged as a ceaseless monologue directed to me, for she sat beside me in the dayroom and made to me, day after day, a series of confessions to which I answered "Yes, I see, yes, I see, I know how you feel," and such was the power of her obsessive talking that I found myself caught up in a life of love affairs in strange beds in back-country hotels, double whiskies, beatings, grief, squalor to the refrain spoken half in amazement half in conviction. "But I loved him at the time."

Nothing mattered in Hilary's life beside her search for him, whoever he might be.

Geoffrey? A drunken miner on the Wild West Coast. Peter? A commercial traveler (described in the directory as a Comm. Agent) selling sweater sets pokerwork bookmarks lingerie, novelties like miniature snowstorms and Japanese paper flowers that open, like truth, without persuasion if put in the element most suited to them. Harry? "Just the opposite of Peter. He's quiet and dark and will go steady." Harry, she assured me, was the one man in her life now. She had met him at one of the hospital dances where romance often sprouted, even in the midst of the sturdy galloping of

The Grand old Duke of York, he had ten thousand men.
He marched them up to the top of the hill and he marched
them down again.

Harry was going to divorce his wife and marry Hilary. "He knows about my past and my drinking and he understands."

She seemed for the moment to have forgotten that Peter also had known about her past and her drinking; he also had understood and had promised to divorce his wife. I felt sympathy for Hilary. She brought to her dedicated desperate search for the "right man" a single-mindedness that would have been a credit to any scientist in his laboratory, yet her haphazard methods of operation and their always tragic aftermath made her a natural target for those, like Sister Bridge and Matron Glass, whose mission was to gather people who had not "learned their lesson" and try to teach it to them or force it upon them or, in the end, advise a "change of personality."

Sometimes to pass the hours Hilary sang in a low husky voice that gave the clean dayroom temporarily the air of a night club. She sang

What do you know, he smiled at me in my dreams last night.
My dreams are getting better all the time.
To think that we were strangers a couple of nights ago . . .

She had reason to sing that her dreams were getting better; she began now to show a subdued restlessness which hinted that the end was in sight. One imagined her passing through this stage in each of her successive affairs, and one felt that each stage and the ritual accompanying it were necessary to provide an exquisite container for her pleasure —a prepared mold for the liquid silver; it was a kind of extended act of love.

One morning Hilary vanished from the laundry where she had pleaded to be allowed to work. Harry also was missing from the male side. Both were found two days later in the thick bush in the hills at the back of the hospital.

It had been a brief cold hungry escapade.

Hilary was put in seclusion and forced to suffer the post-prophetic wisdom of Matron Glass who assured her that she "had it coming to her." Dr. Steward's tall stooped figure could be seen going to the Brick Building to visit the sideroom where she was locked next to Kathleen and

Esme who were in permanent seclusion. After Matron had unlocked the door—such a solemn occasion demanded the presence of the Matron—Dr. Steward entered and began immediately in a prudish apologetic manner to prepare to ask questions.

"Now I don't want you to think, Mrs. Thomas, that we think—"

"Cut the cackle," said Hilary. "I know what you mean. We were going to but we didn't. And anyway I kept thinking of Peter."

"The Commercial Traveler?" queried Dr. Steward swiftly, for Hilary's story was the kind that needed little effort to remember, and although Dr. Steward tried to take an interest in his patients, as far as Matron Glass would let him, and as far as he had the time, the personal details of most patients escaped him unless they were the kind which seemed to have a special retaining power within themselves, like those plastic hooks which attach themselves to the wall without nails or screws.

Dr. Steward, like Dr. Howell before him, had begun as an enthusiastic junior medical officer. He was particularly successful with the young married women for he himself was still young, was married and a father, and believed in giving an atmosphere of intimacy to his few moments of conversation with the patients when he sometimes passed through the ward, by referring with noticeable pride to his wife and family (one small boy). "My wife feels the same way," he would remark. "Yes, my wife suffers like that too."

His references to his wife ranged from menstruation pains to getting up in the morning to seeing strange faces at the window, and though one does not know if his wife approved, the technique at least was successful. When Dr.

Steward had passed through the ward on one of his rare visits, patients could be heard mentioning with pride—even those who were not regarded as "sensible"—that Dr. Steward's wife felt the same way as they did—"He said his wife suffers like this; she feels exactly the way I feel." Or (with amazement and gratitude), "He said that he thinks the same as I do."

The trait for which Dr. Steward became noted, therefore, was his understanding. There were doctors who "got things done" and doctors who cut short whatever you were trying to say to them and doctors who spoke to you in a loud voice as if you couldn't hear properly and doctors who asked you strange questions, but only Dr. Steward dared to admit that he felt "exactly the same way" as you felt. And with this appreciation of his understanding came the urge to protect him, especially from his wife who seemed to be suffering a variety of aches and pains and didn't seem quite right in the head.

"I know he's henpecked," the patients said. "His wife won't let him do a thing."

He was pale, too. Perhaps he was suffering from a secret disease. Hadn't he been in a prison camp in Germany during the war?

Hilary had a special regard for Dr. Steward. She accepted the fact that he had signed her seclusion order, for she knew that he had no protection against Matron Glass and Sister Bridge and the fixed tradition that a patient who escapes is locked in a room and given a bed on the floor. Besides, Hilary had committed the crime of being in the hills for two nights with a man!

Matron Glass was eloquent in her condemnation. Matron Glass herself had nowhere to go at night but the small flat that was provided for her beside Ward One, near the front offices, and on her days off she caught the bus into town or drove her car. Seeing her without her uniform one knew that the uniform and veil were a desperate protection for her—they must have been, for in her tan costume, specially tailored to fit her large body, and her Arch-Comfort tan shoes, she seemed to be stripped of all her power, so much so that she seemed to have an air of helplessness and pathos.

She was an "efficient" matron. She lived for her job. She was stern and eager to teach people lessons and make them "pull themselves together."

After her few weeks of seclusion, when it was found that she wasn't pregnant, Hilary emerged proclaiming herself a changed woman.

"I have had time to think," she said. "It really is Harry that I love. He reminds me of my first boy friend when I was eighteen; the man I should have married; a gentle boy who played cricket on Saturday afternoons in white flannels; and innocent; he blushed mind you, and since when have I seen a man blush for the right reasons? I should have married him."

For a moment it seemed as if in Hilary's mind, excited with sudden memory, the first boy friend had gained over Harry. And then "Harry is his type. Harry has promised to divorce his wife and marry me."

Alas, during Hilary's period of seclusion, Harry had discovered Carol and her "gagement" ring with its "genuine zephyr," and was already thrusting questionable notes through the six-inch opening in the bottom of the dayroom window. He worked on the farm, and passed by every morning and sometimes brought Carol cigarettes as well as loving notes.

Fortunately Hilary was blessed by the gods and at her first dance the following week, before she had had time to ponder the treachery of Harry and the weakness of Carol and her own sadly mistaken judgment of the dark quiet man who would "go steady," she discovered Len. And even had she not discovered him she would not have spent her time pondering; she would have cursed, yes, and if she had been out in the world she would have gone to a beer party, got drunk and met someone else; for in seeking men she was as single minded as a silkworm devouring mulberry leaves.

She could not understand why she had not noticed Len before. He was heavily built, dark, gloomy and sweating, with a thick mustache and toffee-colored eyes. He was "half Italian" and kept thinking he was still in the Italian Campaign in the Second World War, but he was having treatment, and would be cured soon, and then Hilary would be marrying him.

"He's promised. When his divorce goes through—"

> This catling's jungle heart forlorn
> Will die as wild as it was born.
> If I could cage the human race
> And teach it what it is to face
> Never-Get-Out.

There is no need, for we are well enough caged within ourselves, and Custom has turned the key. I can see Dr. Steward running round and round Hilary's cage, telling her to pull herself together, to learn from experience, but not thinking to turn the key that dangles from his watch chain, for surely he needs it himself. "My wife feels the same way . . ."

X

*I*T SEEMED NOW so long ago—it was more than six years—since I had first been in Ward Four and gone out walking and stared curiously and sadly at the crazy people of Ward Two, noting their weird hats, crumpled coats, twisted stockings; and their childish excitement at whatever lay around them; how they pointed ecstatically to the ordinary everyday sun standing habitually in the sky and the flowers that startle with their silence even more than with their color, growing along the garden borders; how they stood, dazzled, at the sight of a figure in shirt sleeves who seemed to them to be the doctor, mowing his front lawn while his wife sat near, dandling their white-haired child.

Now that I belonged to Ward Two I also gaped amazedly at the spectacle of the powerful sun policing the earth, Move On There No Loitering, while the arrested darkness lay dungeoned, awaiting trial. The sun seemed closer, more threatening, with warrants of execution slipped between the shafts of light and placed strategically, like shadows, so that we could read them and take warning, perhaps adopt emergency measures. When I walked with Ward Two it was not the Ward Four sun that stood in the sky, nor the Ward Four flowers that puppeted brightly in the light wind. We saw the sinister collisions of color and heard the explosions along the garden border. We looked with gratitude on the poplar trees and the fear that predisposed them to sudden shiverings reached us through secret channels, causing us to shiver as well. On every occasion I seized the opportunity to walk in the grounds, but Sister Bridge, knowing that I liked to be out under the sky, gave orders that I was not to be "indulged." "Someone who deserves the outing can go," was her verdict. "Someone who knows how to behave herself instead of running screaming from the meal tables and crying if I put her in the dirty dayroom as if she were better than the others when in fact she's worse."

Yet it was the policy of Sister Bridge to encourage everybody from the clean dayroom, and those who could be allowed for a short time from the dirty dayroom, to take part in all official outings—walks, church, dances. Cliffhaven was progressing in its adoption of the "new attitude." In the coat cupboard there hung a collection of ward dresses, pastel-shaded party dresses in stiff shiny materials with gathers pleats and flares and sometimes matching underskirts in parchment nylon, all bought with hospital funds by the Matron on a special expedition to town, and issued for "outings" to those with nothing else to wear, which meant those without visitors. Although Matron Glass was constantly telling me to "write to your people and tell them you need clothes," I did not do so, for my parents either had no money or did not realize that mental patients wear clothes other than the pants which arrived for me in festive parcels at Christmas time and on birthdays.

I was grouped, therefore, with the "forgotten" and with those, also usually "forgotten," who would be in hospital until they died. This grouping had its pleasures. One day we were fitted for new skirts and sweater sets, and their arrival was an exciting event, if one did not think too much about the fact that one had been chosen to wear what could be called the uniform of the dead. I still could not believe there was no hope for me, or I kept running over the rat-infested no man's land between belief and disbelief and pitching camp on one side or the other. I dithered in Time, not knowing what to call forth from the future, fearing to face the present and the cruelty of Sister Bridge and the penances she imposed upon me, and not daring to turn to the past. So I was silent, attacking my time-bordered self, blighting, like black frost, the edges of my life until they crumpled and dropped in the bitter southeast wind from the sea.

Yes, we danced, the crazy people from Ward Two whom even the people from the observation ward and the convalescent ward looked upon as oddities and loonies. We dressed in our exotic party dresses, taffetas and rayons and silk jersey florals, and we lined up outside the clinic to have make-up put on our faces from the ward box with its stump of lipstick, coated and roughened powder puffs, box of blossom-pink powder and scent bottle squirting carnation scent behind our ears (who did we expect to kiss them) and in the hollow of our wrists. By the time we were ready we were a garden of carnations and we looked like stage whores.

There was excitement, a sweating pleasantness and promise which made our noses shine in spite of the slapped-on powder puff, and slowly dampened and stained the underarms of our dresses. Matron would arrive, breathless and pink cheeked and tell us, like a messenger bearing news from a far country, that "Ward Four were ready ages ago and have gone through to the hall" or "Ward One are just going through" or "The band has arrived." This would only increase the excitement and those who simmered over beyond control would have to be skimmed away to bed, and others reduced by cold threats to a reasonable calm. Matron Glass would smile, and Sister Bridge would smile and compliment us on our appearance and warn Carol about getting with her partner into dark corners of the men's dining room where we were to have our supper, and it would at last be time to go across the dark yard that was wet with dewfall, through Ward One with its smell of wet cots and scabbed skin and the personal smell, the passport or free sample that death provides for old women, along the visitors' corridor with its prison atmosphere, barred fire, brown polished linoleum and long leather seats with upright backs, through to the unfamiliar part of the hospital, to the dreariness and barrenness that are peculiar to the men's wards; and at last to the Big Hall with its bright lights and powdered floor, and along the walls the seats half-filled on one side with men and on the other side with women, and down at the back, facing the stage, the red plush armchairs for the officials—the doctors and perhaps visitors invited from town to see mental patients engaged in recreation. The officials usually arrived a short while before supper, and the doctor present would be the one on duty.

The band sat on the stage, making lightheaded preliminary music. We found places against the wall. The lights dazzled. "Istina, Edith will look after you," Edith would say, half-pulling me to a seat. "You sit beside Edith." When the last group from the male side had arrived, looking self-conscious with slicked-down hair and pressed trousers and white handkerchiefs peeping from pockets, and when the last group of women entered—the blasé convalescents from the Cottage, exclaiming petulantly that they didn't really want to go dancing but their ward sister had made them and anyway they thought they'd see what all the fuss was about, then it was time to begin.

I couldn't help staring at the Ward Four people who looked opulent in their own clothes, Mrs. Pilling wearing jewelry and Mabel in the glistening moth-eaten evening dress which she always wore as the partner of Dick the patient in white tie and tails and white gloves.

The band started a waltz.

"Nice and old-fashioned," a nurse said. "Get up and dance, everyone."

The men either stood rigidly against the wall or rushed helter-skelter across the room to clasp a partner and whirl her away to dance with or without her consent. Sometimes one of the men, having chosen his partner and danced a few steps with her, decided she did not suit him after all, and he would walk away and partner someone else; sometimes a woman ran across the room to choose her man. There were few ballroom formalities and much of the "plain-speaking" that makes a virtue of insult; there were endearments and pledges and muddled conversations following the first remark which was not, "A good floor isn't it?" but "How long have you been here?"

Most of the patients who had been in hospital a long time had their faithful partner. Mine was Eric, a middle-aged balding man who reminded me strangely of a conjurer who used to visit us at school at the end of the term and charged us threepence to see him spread satin cloths over the classroom table and draw silk handkerchiefs from a top hat, and who, although he never performed a complicated miracle like cutting people in half or climbing a rope to the ceiling of the classroom, could always be relied upon to make no mistakes with the satin cloth and the silk handkerchiefs.

Eric was unromantic, but he kept in time with the music and he did not tread on my feet. His mouth hung open, his head was thrust forward and his brow glistened with the oil of endeavor and concentration. I waited patiently for him to perform a miracle just as I had waited for the school conjurer after I had staked my threepence; nothing but satin cloths and silk handkerchiefs; the face of the world stayed the same, the sick were not healed, the roof did not dissolve and let in the stars.

Eric taught me to dance. We danced the Destiny,

My dear I love you so
Just pack up your trousseau . . .

He was pedantic and fatherly and usually took me to supper and we ate steadily, like reading a book and not missing a single word, through the sandwiches to the scrumptious cakes with fancy icing until the drinks arrived, bloating and vivid and fizzy, one bottle each, or two if you were cunning or had an enterprising partner. All romance was abandoned for the feed. I remember one partner who did not open his mouth except to eat and to say to me, before passing from the sandwiches to the cakes, "After this I'll feel your leg."

Our hearts beat fast with sheer greed at the sight of the food; there was always a feverish stowing of sandwiches into pockets and a pang of regret when the last few dances were beginning and we had to leave the remains of the supper and return to the Hall. We would be tired now, for it was almost ten o'clock, yet our excitement which was fast turning to irritability became renewed when we caught sight of Dr. Steward and perhaps Dr. Portman sitting in their plush chairs watching and pointing and smiling.

Always when I saw the doctor my heart contracted with suspense, for in spite of the influence of Matron Glass and Sister Bridge it was the doctor's decision which mattered —yet how could he decide if he didn't know you, didn't really know you except to say in Ward Four "Good Morning," and in Ward Two, nothing, and listen only to Sister Bridge asserting that what you needed was a lesson to teach you how to behave and pull yourself together, a girl with your education. So when I was whirled in a waltz past the royal dais I would tremble with apprehension and try to dance well, and think "There's Dr. Steward, he's watching me, he's seeing that someone has asked me to dance, that I'm not a wallflower, he's seeing that I'm well, that I needn't be in Ward Two spending all day shut in the dayroom or the yard or the park; he's deciding about me. Deciding now." But when I came closer to him and dared to sneak a glance at him sitting in royalty there, it appeared that he wasn't thinking about me at all, that he hadn't even noticed me, he was talking to someone, saying "Yes, I . . . I . . . I . . ."

Of course. Like me, like all of us, he was thinking and talking about himself.

The dance ended, we were lined up in ward groups at the entrance to the hall, and hustled out, with the nurse tapping our shoulder as we passed, counting us. "Come along or you'll be here all night. Come along. Any more for Ward Two? Nurse, have you got your correct number? Have you checked them?" When we hurried noisily through Ward One some of the children woke up and began to cry at the lights and the hubbub of voices, and some stayed undisturbed, blissful and rosy with sleep. The old ladies stirred and sighed; their beds and their bones creaked. Without ceremony, once we had reached the Brick Building, we were stripped of our party dresses and put into our room or our dormitory and locked in.

I wonder who made the decision to provide us with cakes instead of sedatives or if a choice was ever given. Cakes were plentiful. Almost every night, and particularly the night of a dance or any other official outing there was little hope of sleep amid the screams and shouts and curses. Our noisy return after a dance would awaken the few people in the dirty dormitory who ever slept; the others would continue their raging on a less subdued note. And those returning irritable and tired, not wanting to go to bed and depressed at the thought of tomorrow and the sight of the beautiful party dresses being borne away anyhow by the night nurses acting as cruel bailiffs, were too easily roused to anger and violence.

I huddled in my small room with my head under the bedclothes and my fingers to my ears and my eyes stinging with rejected sleep, and too soon morning came, the blackbirds, the dim light through the closed shutters, and the six o'clock jingling of keys as the nurses unlocked the doors and threw in the clothing bundles. There were fights, clothing was missing, people felt stale and sticky with old make-up on their faces and gaped like clowns at one another in the sorting out of oneself and other people that is part of the difficult routine of emerging from a half-sleep and acknowledging morning. The staff too suffered from irritability. "No more dances for you my lady, no more dances for you."

And all day among those who talked the conversation would be of the dance. Brenda would purse her lips and say, "I saw you last night Miss Istina Mavet, having a wonderful time dancing and dancing. You had such a *dashing* partner. How I wish I were you to have a dashing partner to make my heart beat. Get out of here Mr. Frederick Barnes. This instant."

Eric wasn't "dashing" and I hadn't been enjoying a "wonderful time" yet Brenda's attitude to me was always one of sympathetic envy and longing which made me feel responsible for her rescue and for her plight if rescue never came. I was ashamed of my wholeness compared with Brenda's fragmented mind scattered by secret explosion to the four corners of itself. I knew they had tried without success to bore holes in her brain to let the disturbing forces fly out, like leaves or demons from a burning tree. Who could make her whole? Where was the conjurer? I was powerless. I knew only a rotund cleric who might, on persuasion, produce a stream of silk handkerchiefs from a top hat.

XI

A SPORTS DAY WAS held each year in February, late summer, when the fresh sea breezes, already seeking signs of decay, combed irreverently through the grass inspecting each withered blade like the young pointing out in public the gray hairs on an aging head, and thumbed each leaf like hired scrutineers counting the votes for death. Often for days on end, out of caution or inertia and the need to gather secret weapons, the season stayed poised in the same weather, bringing a deceptive feeling of timelessness, a separation from time which was, in reality, time's invasion which could not be borne and so was rejected from consciousness and remained monotonously in the background, unnoticed, like a clock ticking or traffic or the sea flowing.

When Sports Day was held at this time it always gave a feeling of shock by its intrusion. One was forced to stop and listen, as when the rhythm of the clock or the traffic or the sea changes; and fear came, as if the bolstering background of time had suddenly dissolved. It seems strange now that so many emotions could be aroused by a mere Sports Day, and that when the season was tired, in dressing gown and pinned hair, so to speak, in preparation for the compulsion of sleep, the mentally ill should be called forth to build a temple glorifying physical power. What did it mean?

Nothing. It was simply Sports Day, another finishing post in a marathon of excitement which had begun weeks before and from which, one by one, the patients who became uncontrollable were dropped out, put in the park or the yard or the dirty dayroom or in seclusion; while Matron Glass and Sister Bridge stood by the side of this track of restlessness and agitation barracking us with cries of, "No Sports Day for you my lady misbehaving like this. Watch your step or Monday won't see you at the Sports."

In the week end before the Day the temple and its precincts were marked on the lawn in front of the main door of the hospital: white lines, jumping poles, sandpits, red and white flags cheekily slapping the air; and that Sunday on our walk we saw groups of men patients rehearsing the chief ceremonies—vaulting over poles, jumping in sacks, or limbering up, running on the spot with high knee-raising. They were like little boys who take the field before or after the big game and hope the crowd is watching their exploits; but in this case the men were not imitating the heroes of the hour: they were imitating themselves, and the circle of their isolation was complete.

Watch me. I jump so high I reach the sky.

On Monday we dressed in our party clothes which looked gaudy and incongruous on people about to take part in sports, yet it was the hospital rule that all patients visiting the front of the hospital were to be "dressed," as village folk sometimes came as spectators, and on the second day of the Sports the children of the village were given a half-holiday, and a special programme of races, followed by a spree of soft drinks and sweets, was arranged for them.

We stood around in our sweat-smelling creased clothes watching the people from Ward One being lined up by the attendant in his smart black suit with its cuffless trousers like those worn by a policeman, and some of us volunteered to take part, for the longer you had been in hospital the more willing you became to join in festivities that to the uninitiated, like most of Ward Four and the convalescent ward, brought only embarrassment and self-consciousness, so that few of these people could be persuaded to jump about in sacks and knot handkerchiefs around their ankles and run with the men in the three-legged race. As at the dance, they "wondered what the fuss was about."

But we in Ward Two and those permanent patients of Ward One, living in a time of prolonged war, moved closer to one another in spite of our separately sealed worlds, like glass globes of trick snowstorms, and we unself-consciously grabbed any pleasures and did not really care if we ran with taffeta dresses tucked into our pants, and were not ashamed to present ourselves for two ice creams, lying that we had been "missed out" at the time of the first distribution. Someone called through a loudspeaker, "Women's flat race!" and set my heart thumping with excitement, for after the preliminary exchange, "You're not bad at running, Istina, why don't you enter?"—"No, I don't think so."—"Why not? Keep up the reputation of the ward."—"All right then."—I knew I would hurry across to the starting point and when the pistol shot sounded, leap into the white-bordered lane and run for dear life though the wind kept blowing in my face and trying to prevent my advance, and I would feel as if I were making no progress over the ground that seemed to shift strangely in heavy clots like wet sand.

Sometimes I snapped first across the tape and hurried breathless and proud, and certain that everyone was admiring me, to the attendant who gave me a card printed in red ink FIRST PLACE; and with the other prize winners, all of us talking together with our words lopping out like white of egg that is in two minds about which globule to join and strays between one and the other, half-fusing with both, I stopped under the flap of the sawdust-smelling tent where the prizes were arranged on trestle tables. Displayed and pleased, we surrendered our tickets. Eric, as one of the trusted patients—and somehow as a natural inhabiter of the small tents that, offering seedy forms of magic, encircle like off-white canvas alps the fairground of a traveling side show—stood behind one of the tables, distributing the prizes.

"I watched you," he said as he handed me the nylon stockings, first prize. "Come with me in the three-legged."

"No," I replied distantly. "I've promised Ted."

Ted was the former Borstal boy who now worked in the Superintendent's garden and helped with the milk cans in the morning. He was stocky and dark and his face seemed always to have an expression of crafty admiration both for himself and for other people. It was the overwhelming desire to touch what he admired that had sent him to the Borstal reformatory. His hands were clumsy and large, like separate people with wills of their own, and to deny them the power to touch would be like denying a sculptor his contact with stone. But Ted was not a sculptor; he was a young man with a love of admiring and of being admired, and his cunning expression arose from his continual need to practice the commerce of admiration in which he had truly invested his life.

On Sports Day he entered for many races, and won, and could not contain his high spirits but leapt about the field getting in everyone's way, and when he came to me, I said yes I would go with him in the three-legged race. We won. I made another journey to the tent to collect my prize.

"I watched you," Eric said as he handed me the nylon stockings. "Will you come with me next year in the three-legged?"

Meanwhile the drinks had arrived, not bottled fizz as at the dances but what looked like kerosene tins brimming with blood-colored liquid, a heavy syrupy brew which was distributed in hospital cups and left a red stain inside the cup. We drank and returned for more; we were allowed to drink as much as we liked, and the absence of anyone saying "Young lady, you've had your whack," gave us a gaudy feeling of delight and perhaps, on the outskirts of our mind, stirred a slumbering apprehension at the thought of the inevitable aftermath of our makeshift picnic pleasures. Gaily we let ourselves be herded back to the ward for dinner, and were shocked to see that Ward Two had not changed, that people still screamed and cursed in the dirty dayroom, and Sister Bridge still called out, "Lavatory Ladies!" standing on guard outside the bathroom door.

It is always hard to believe that the will to change something does not produce an immediate change. Why did Ward Two still exist when we had been merrily carousing on the front lawn, filling ourselves with ruby syrup and ice cream in the atmosphere of a fairground? Why did we imagine that because we watched only the stream of silk handkerchiefs, the conjurer was not still practicing his skills of deceit, so that in the end we refused to believe in the deceit?

In the afternoon the doctors and their wives and children visited the Sports to watch the races between members of the staff. We ran no more races; we were spectators now, gazing intensely at the strange people who were not patients. We began to feel lonely and depressed as the excitement of our share of the sports faded, as it flowed away leaving the dregs of ordinary routine, Brick Ladies, Lavatory Ladies, Park Ladies. We knew the truth of picnics and dances and sports days, just as a child, after a while, knows the truth when the dentist promises to take away the pain by putting "a little dolly on a dolly's pillow to sleep in your mouth."

XII

*M*Y HANDS MY hands are not clean the bitten fingernails ingrained with dirt and my beard that began to grow when I was in Lawn Lodge grows more quickly now, yet no one, I think, suspects that I have a beard. I rub it off with a sandpaper mitt which my family sends me, and one of the perils of my life is to hide these mitts on my person without anyone knowing and to scrape my face with them each morning under the bedclothes.

I am vain. I am growing thin. I look at myself in the mirror in the corridor, at my ward skirt and ward sweater set, and my frizzy hair. I am twenty-eight; it is nearly eight years since I first came to Ward Four. Across the sea a king has died and a pall was thrown over the music and Carol cried out for the dirges to end their all-day flowing from the radio on its caged and locked shelf, and for *Some Enchanted Evening* to be played.

Some enchanted evening you may see a stranger.

And a Queen has been crowned, with compulsory celebrations in all the wards, parties and more feasts. Brenda played the piano in the clean dayroom although Mr. Frederick Barnes refuses to leave her alone at all now and does not wish her to play the piano any more and her going against his wishes produces afterwards appalling violence, recriminations, in the domestic life of her mind. On that day we drank flat muddy beer, and Carol sang for us, *Some Enchanted Evening*, and *Walking my Baby Back Home*, and Hilary sang

> *On top of Old Smoky all covered in snow*
> *I lost my true lover through courting so slow.*

Minnie Cleave played *The Campbells Are Coming*, and was in smiles because she had found her handkerchief; and after some encouragement Mrs. Shaw danced, for she had enormous breasts which hung down like empty wineskins almost to her knees and the patients and nurses found amusement in watching them flop up and down when she danced. And Maudie, who was God, seeing the popularity of Mrs. Shaw's item, volunteered to dance also, a skipping measure, pointing her toes and showing her well-shaped legs that would have graced the knee breeches of a courtier. She quickly became breathless, but continued prancing.

"Stop it Maudie," shouted Carol.

Maudie extends her punitive arm. "Down you go," she warned, becoming God.

"Now," said the nurse, "who else will give an item for Coronation Day?"

"I could tell a story," began Big Betty wickedly, "but not in company."

"Julie, what about you?" a nurse suggested. "Sing for us."

"No," said bearded Julie shortly.

Then the matron and Dr. Steward arrived and both gave

a general smile around the room, an indulgent smile. Matron addressed Big Betty who was reclining on her sofa. "Well Betty, enjoying yourself?"

"It's these young things," said Big Betty, "They just won't perform for the Coronation."

"It's not every day the Queen is crowned," the matron said sanctimoniously. "Now you people do justice to the event and celebrate."

Sun and shade are tricks and I trust nothing and I understand why we fear the telephone, why, although we have cut the cables, we still lift the receiver and wait for the voice we dread; and I understand mirrors and try to track the point in their depth when we become nothing—yes, I look in the tall mirror in the corridor outside the sister's office and I know it is set there to trap us, like the mirrors in the department stores, that the house detective may catch us picking over the haberdashery of ourselves and shoplifting. Who owns us now? Is it our crime that we steal from ourselves? But I have never seen so much love in the storehouse; confined and sealed and lowered in price, it seeps and fumes through the wall as a mephitic presence; one wipes the trace of it like a mist from the mirror.

And they say forever now, yes my lady you'll never get out of here so you'd better make up your mind to accept things; as if I were a jumble sale, as if I were my own charity. I do not have E.S.T. nor have I had it at all since I left Treecroft, and although the dread of it is still there it is distant; besides, the doctor has promised. Yet daily the hopelessness increases. I try to make a history-book treaty with the sun, laying down, for others to learn, its conditions of shining whereby each day the burned sky is grafted with new cloud; it is hard to communicate forgiveness. In the morning the sun breathes lemon vapor on the lawn and the planks in the park fence are stained with the dampness of night. Is the sun, the boiler house, a secret crematorium?

In the ward office at the back of the right-hand side of the drawer Sister Bridge keeps the box of barbiturate tablets which should, by regulation, be locked in the poison cupboard. I have seen them. I saw them one evening when Sister Bridge was off duty and her deputy, Nurse Clake, said to me "Istina will you massage my legs and feet."

I am afraid of Nurse Clake. She is married to a butcher and both she and her husband have caught in their faces the red glare of the meat. What is to prevent me from sneaking to the office, on my way from the dining room, snatching the tablets, swallowing them, and falling into a deep sleep and never waking again?

Death I said; but it is like truth and from continent to continent we fly within the two words, first-class in the comfort of them, but when it is time for us to leave the words themselves and parachute to their meaning in the dark earth and seas below us, the parachute fails to open, we are stranded or drift wide of our target or, peering over into the darkness and stricken with fright, we refuse to leave the comfort of the words.

I wrote to death; Dear Death, I said, formalizing our relationship, and the leavings of light wastefully spilled were strewn on the lawn and the park. I stole the tablets.

"Bitch to try and get me sacked; bitch I know why you stole."

Then a stomach pump, black coffee, before I slept a

screaming screaming at Sister Bridge leaning, her hair stacked and wired like straw; then sleep in seclusion.

Then morning. Breakfast for Esme and Kathleen and the sound of the empty enamel bowls being thrown against the door, and I waited for my bowl of porridge, slice of bread and mug of tea but nobody visited my room. I heard the babble of the workers from Ward One and at half-past eight the people being brought from the clean dayroom to their work in the Brick Building; Hilary singing "If I were a Blackbird" and outside in the yard the twins, who communicated like dogs, barking to each other.

Suddenly a nurse opened my door and thrust in a dressing gown and slippers. "Put these on."

I could feel my heart beating faster and my breath getting out of step with itself and panic overcoming me and I tried to remember my secret rule which I had formulated in order to maintain my sanity.

I forbid you Istina Mavet to panic in a small locked room.

A nurse appeared with a wheelchair; there were two other nurses in the background. I had to be cunning.

"I'll walk," I said, and I might have said just as calmly I'll fly I'll go by Harpy by bat strung on silk by plastic plate by kangaroo by word by tourist bacterium.

I had to be so cunning.

"Let me walk by myself," I said, and could not speak any more, having used my ration of calm; and with three nurses surrounding me I walked from the Brick Building along the road to the observation ward. For treatment. Just as I was passing the clean dayroom I seized my chance and rushed at the window smashing the glass with my head; there was a splitting and splintering of ice and the roving fish, smelling blood, swung about and nosed forward. The lifeguards lay on the beach, making love; the air was heavy with tons of light.

My face was bleeding. I was in the wheelchair, in the treatment room. I climbed on the bed and closed my eyes.

"Let me see," said Dr. Steward, sponging the blood.

I began to cry. "You promised. You promised."

I woke in the small locked room where I lay on a mattress on the floor, with canvas blankets and sheets, and for many days I stayed there, in seclusion.

I smelled the room, I went shopping among the smells —old urine mixed with misery for it was not the honest stench of babies not yet trained but a preserved and outcast adult smell of those who had known and been deprived of their knowing; the smell of stale polish, straw and straw dust, sunlessness; the smell of corners, of the wooden door that had been kicked and hammered upon for seventy years.

Every morning I was given a bath (a rule for patients in seclusion), my room was quickly cleaned (usually by Carol with a wet mop) my bed was made, and by the time I had returned shivering from the cold wind that blew along the concrete stairway and through the wire-netting doors of the Brick Building to the doorless bathroom with its exposed yellow-stained old baths, I was ready to be locked in for the day. My breakfast had consisted of a bowl of porridge and one or two thick slices of bread with yellow coracles of butter scooped on it where the butter had been too cold to spread; and a cup or enamel mug of swilly tea with parcels floating on it, and secret messages in the dregs at the bottom. My breakfast always tasted sweeter than any feast, for the first reason that it meant *no treatment,* for ever since the doctor had not kept his promise and they had seized me to take me to Ward Four, part of my day and night was spent in anxious planning how I should avoid the next attempt at E.S.T., yet at the same time I had to force myself to obey my rule never to panic in a small locked room.

My breakfast was company. Sometimes I saved half to eat later in the morning when the workers, with their hustle and bustle and swish of their mops and echoes of song and conversation, had gone from the Brick Building and all was quiet except for Zoe's mumbling. Zoe did not sleep in a room or a dormitory but in a recess at the end of the corridor as if she had emerged as some pitiful human spawn from the Brick Building itself. She was in bed forever. She had little flesh, only great prehistoric bones that jutted out of the wrapping blanket when they led her to the bathroom, and her face was like one of those maps that are the postmortem of the earth's yesterday that show the strata faults and folds brought about by natural disaster or time or simply by being.

All morning the building was quiet, for Esme and Kathleen were sometimes taken into the yard. I heard the distant screams and cries from the park, and I thought, perhaps it is time to eat my bread and butter for company. Once a small mouse came running in such a hurry underneath my door and over to my bed and on to the clothes. I gasped with fright and moved and the gray mouse ran back under the door. But he returned. He came again and again. I christened him Mr. Griffiths, for I noted that he was a Brick Building and Mattress Shed mouse and therefore civilized. How civilized? Well he did not hop like a field mouse but ran, as civilized people must run in order to get to the end and find out why they were running. I established a precarious friendship with Mr. Griffiths for, although he would not tell me about his own world, he listened, bribed first like any human being with headlines promises and breakfast crumbs, to my story of Ward Two and E.S.T. and Sister Bridge who had given orders that I was to have no books or writing materials and that no one was to talk to me.

But one of the nurses pushed a magazine for me through the slit in the corner of the wall and another sneaked me a pencil. The magazine, called *Woman's Life*, was busy with startling serials about doctors and nurses, malaria and rubber shares, with matrimonial advice, and Night Thoughts By The Man-With-Gray-Eyes, and advertisements for bile beans and a pull-out supplement of symmetrical jellies, and polychromatic cooking, and knitting and sewing patterns. I read *Woman's Life*, poring compulsively over the advertisements as if they contained the secrets of life and freedom (some promised both, in a twenty-eight days' supply), and reading every line in the absorbed way that I used to read the squares of newspaper that my father cut for the lavatory at home. With the pencil I wrote on the wall snatches of remembered poems but the pencil applied to the Brick Building wall was like a revolutionary dye that refuses to "take"; the two elements were antagonistic and the words suffered the cruelty of indistinctness or, out of self-defense, they preferred to remain aloof, unformed.

"Here," Sister Bridge said, "is a basin of water a cloth and soap. Rub the writing from the wall."

How many miles to Babylon?

Deprived of my pencil and my magazine which was discovered in the making of my bed, I recited poems to myself or sang or, silent, remembered and feared. Esme and Kathleen were quiet. Esme, if she was not put in the yard or park, spent all day crouched in the corner of the room with her nightie over her head. She was wild and would rush at anyone who entered—anyone except Sister Bridge. Kathleen was fierce too and had the distinction of a visitor every fortnight—her mother. Once a fortnight then Kathleen was dressed, her nose was wiped, her hair tied with a ribbon, her swollen hardened feet put into shoes that had been bought years ago yet were still brand new, as your shoes would be if you wore them for eight hours each year. Kathleen used to stand still all day except for an occasional sudden stamping of her feet, the way a horse stamps to get rid of flies and irritations when it is standing alone in a paddock.

My skin was smoothing itself over my bones settling into the hollows and curves subsiding like a new road unused to the strain of traffic; pockets appeared, I was growing thin; I had bitten all my fingernails and had no half moons. Sometimes I remembered the magazine with its vivid jelly, and when in my mind I was tired of climbing the ruby crags and slopes and sinking in the transparent valleys, I would sleep, with my head under the harsh canvas blanket, and would be awakened at half-past eleven by the sound of the dinner van arriving at the door of Ward One with the stew or roast and the can of lentil or pea soup.

Then I would hear the Ward Two door being unlocked and locked, the yard gate being unlocked and locked, the door to the Brick Building being unlocked, and the arrival sounds of dinner, a bowl of stew and a bowl of rice, but no bread for Mr. Griffiths or as company for my afternoon. Half-past three—teatime—two sausages, bread and butter, a beautiful slice of rainbow cake which I gluttonously ate, saving a small piece of bread and butter and thinking that if ever I was allowed outside "in the world" I would be thrown, as we who do not starve are thrown, into a confused crowd of tastes and have only the memory of the private sacramental taste of bread.

And now the people from the dirty dayroom would be driven across to the Brick Building; screaming, cursing, bedsteads being bumped, doors being battered, cries and quarrels that would not cease all night or even in the morning. I heard Violet, with her usual screams at a higher pitch than the others, and knew she would be standing with her fingers plugged in her ears, trying not to listen to the voices, and her eyes closed, trying not to watch the terrifying black figures with faces like fleas that moved backwards and forwards, buying and selling, all night.

And then I would have to hide under my bedclothes and block my own ears because Bertha was in the room next to me. I heard them dragging her along the corridor; and as they passed outside she escaped and switched my light on and off and thrust through the peephole a scrap of paper torn from the front page of the *Mail* which read Real Estate Shipping news and one death, Mr. Humphrey Noke. I put the paper under my pillow for future study. Mr. Humphrey Noke had requested no flowers. He was forty and a patient sufferer and mourned by his loving wife and his undertakers were Causeway and Mead, Ltd.

All night Bertha sang one song, *Nearer My God to Thee,* and raved on and on about what she called "the shock treatment" and held conversations with the doctor who had never spoken to her except to say Good Morning and even that was an economical greeting intended for all the patients in the clean dayroom. Bertha stayed in the room all day now and still sang *Nearer My God to Thee* and I knew that, although one can be charitable at a distance, it is more difficult when one shares a corridor in day-and-night seclusion with the neighbor who is to be pitied. I planned to kill Bertha, to silence her; day and night her voice stayed in my ears and crawled along the skin of my face and penetrated the roots of my hair. I clenched my fists and cried for her to stop singing. Her voice sprang at me from the corners of the room and flowed from the dim light in the battered cage near the ceiling. I heard her spitting. "Doctor Doctor," she cried, "Nearer My God to Thee, nearer to Thee."

After some days they took her away for treatment and she returned smiling. "I had the shock treatment," she said placidly.

She was allowed to return to the clean dayroom where she would remain until the familiar signs began again—the switching and smashing of the lights, the talk of "the shock treatment," the singing of *Nearer My God to Thee*.

Bertha's singing incensed Maudie who was God and did not think she should be thus addressed. Maudie was tall, well built, middle aged. Her hair was silver, her voice deep and powerful. She was God. She would stand in the dayroom pointing her finger menacingly at anyone who happened to annoy her.

"Down you go Carol Page," she commanded. "Down you go. It is God speaking."

"You're not God. You're a silly old woman," Carol would

taunt, at the same time turning to the other patients and half-stating, half-questioning, "She's not God, is she?"

For in spite of her pose of being grown up and her "gagement" ring with the genuine zephyr and her bullying command of most of the patients in the dayroom, Carol was a credulous child, full of superstitions fears and perplexities. She was afraid of words and could not grasp them entirely. If one watched her in conversation one could see her cower as the words, some quite simple, that she could not yet understand or pronounce, came tumbling towards her, seeming to gather impetus like falling boulders with the power to kill. It was brave of Carol to stand and not flee and try to grasp the outsize words that she needed to give her the stature denied her by her dwarfed body.

Was Maudie God? Carol was never sure, for the minister in church had said that although God was in heaven he was also everywhere, spying on you to write your name in his book. Carol believed the minister. She always went up to him afterwards, to shake hands with him in the same way that she went to the lady visitors to get reassurance from them and tell them about her "gagement ring" and her being "jitimate."

"Down you go!" Maudie shouted. "Down you go, damn you."

Then she would lift her ward skirt and dance a clean-dayroom version of the cancan; to her this seemed not inconsistent with the behavior of God.

For many weeks I stayed in seclusion sleeping on the floor with the cold wind rushing its draught in my face, and Mr. Griffiths calling now and again for his bread and butter. I had blankets now; I liked being alone and snug, thinking about Mr. Griffiths and wondering about Mr. Humphrey Noke. Who was he? Why did he die? What was the conversation of the worms as they considered his dead face?

A visitor came for me. Mystified I dressed in the crumpled clothes they gave me and was led by the nurse into the clinic where someone waited surrounded by the bottles and specimens and masks and gowns. It was Eunice. I had met her twice before in my life, and she had wanted to help me. I burst into tears. I was sitting now, on a small hard clinic chair, like a chair in a classroom. The nurse stayed with me.

"I was told you weren't allowed visitors," Eunice began, "but I pleaded, and they let me in for a few minutes. Is there anything you want?"

"Humphrey Noke is dead," I whispered. "I didn't want him to die."

She looked puzzled. She did not say Cheer up. She was dressed in black.

"Humphrey Noke is dead," I repeated.

"I remember you used to like him," she said quickly, and from her handbag she drew a snapshot.

"This is for you. Henry James's house in Rye."

"You have to go now," the nurse told Eunice. We said goodbye. My clothes were taken from me and I returned to the dingy sour room with my tiny snapshot of Henry James's house warm against my hand.

XIII

*O*NE MORNING I WAS given my clothes and told to get up. My clothes flapped and sucked at my bones like a tent pitched in the snow to shelter the dead explorers from the blizzard as if the dead in their coldness need shelter from cold in the same way that man needs most to hide from the attributes which make him human.

After being for weeks in the small shuttered room I blinked in the harsh gritty sulphur-colored daylight as I followed the nurse out into the park amongst the patients from the dirty dayroom, and sat there on the grass and looked up at the sky at the clouds walking the plank of light. Suddenly the park gate was unlocked and someone entered; it was a doctor I had never seen before, a short man with a monkey-like face and his head on one side and his white coat too long. I stared at him, everybody stared at him, for no doctor ever came into the park. Didn't he know that doctors could not mingle in this way with the disturbed patients, that even if Matron Glass approved of his lone touring of the ward, and it was certain that she did not approve, he would surely be mobbed by women pleading to go home although they knew nobody wanted them and there was nowhere for them to go; yet they would keep asking, "When can I get out of here, out of this dump?"

The strange doctor walked slowly into the park and at once was surrounded by women talking to him and taking his arm, and it was astonishing that he took their arms, and talked to them and laughed. He did not reprimand anyone, saying, "Pull down your dress," when some of the patients lifted their dress to show him, and he did not inquire if missing stockings had been thrust down the lavatory bowl or shoes thrown over the fence. No, he talked and listened with respect and did not seem afraid or hurried or disconcerted in case Matron Glass surprised him walking unescorted in the park among the disturbed patients who were now crowding to him like children to an ice-cream seller on a hot day or like people in lonely outposts wanting news.

"Hello," he said to me. "What if I bring you some pictures to look at? Will you tell me stories about them? I hear you've been very naughty."

I burst into tears. So everybody, even the new doctor called me naughty as if I were a child in disgrace. I ran from him to the top of the park and lay on the grass considering my crime and turning the imitation judgment that everyone, even myself, seemed to treasure and no one could part with, like an evil jewel in my hand.

At dinner Carol told us that the new doctor was Dr. Trace. "I told him about my 'gagement ring,'" she said.

A few days later Dr. Steward asked to interview me in the clinic.

"We don't like to see you here," he said. "There's an

operation which changes the personality and reduces the tension, and we've decided it would be best for you to have the operation. One of your parents will sign the paper. We've asked your mother to come for an interview."

There was a staccato thudding in my chest and I seemed to be falling away from myself like a tree that, having stood many years in a caverned reserve of personal space, is suddenly felled yet leaves, still upright, the force of its habitual life, like an invisible shape withstanding the greedy inrush of air.

Ha, I thought. I felt myself being packed in layers of ice and I shivered.

Dr. Steward's eyes loped up and down like seals in a round pool.

"You will be changed," he repeated. "The tension will be reduced."

His Adam's apple bulged like plumbing in his throat. His face was gray. "The prison camp in Germany," I thought, and then Miss Dock, the history teacher who wove in her spare time and made baskets and raffia stands for teapots, switched on her face before me like a light and battered the title like a neon advertisement, *Europe in the Melting Pot*. She smiled with glee and poured in the liquid continents and islands and stirred the mixture while Dr. Steward Matron Glass Sister Bridge prepared the new mold.

"What will they do?" I asked.

"It's an operation on the brain of course," said Dr. Steward.

Of course.

I remembered a picture of the brain, how it looked like

a shelled walnut and its areas were marked in heavy print, Concentration, Memory, Emotion, like the names of cities in a strange allegorical land.

"I want to go home," I said. I did not mean to where my parents were living or to any other house of wood stone or brick. I felt no longer human. I knew I would have to seek shelter now in a hole in the earth or a web in the corner of a high ceiling or a safe nest between two rocks on an exposed coast mauled by the sea. In the rush of loneliness which overcame me, at the doctor's words, I found no place to stay, nowhere to cling like a bat from a branch or spin a milk-white web about a thistle stalk.

"The tension will be reduced," Dr. Steward repeated in formal tones, like someone announcing the departure of a train.

Then he smiled, "It's better than staying here all the time, isn't it? Now run along and be good."

After my mother had signed the paper giving consent to the operation, and everything was being arranged, Sister Bridge began to show kindness towards me.

"With your personality changed," she said, "no one will dream your were what you were. So many patients have had this operation or are going to have it. I know one woman who was here for twenty years and now—what do you think?—she's selling hats in one of the fashion stores in town. And she used to be in seclusion, like you."

"I don't think I could sell hats," I said doubtfully.

"You've no idea what you'll be able to do. You'll be out of hospital in no time instead of spending your life here as otherwise you'll have to do, my lady, and you'll get a good job in a shop or perhaps an office, and you'll never regret having had a lobotomy."

Now that my personality had been condemned, like a slum dwelling, the planners were at work. The nurses were given permission to talk to me, and they and Sister Bridge, even Matron Glass, moved into my "changed" personality like immigrants to a new land staking their claim.

In fact this prospect of acquiring another person's virgin mind, like a share in a sudden fortune, brought a confused excitement of planning and speculation, so that day after day I was confided in and spoken kindly to with sentences that invariably began, "When you are changed . . ."

I felt remote from the arrangements being made for me; as if I were lying on my death bed watching the invasion of my house and the disposal of my treasures and glimpsing through the half-open door into the adjoining room the waiting coffin—my final burrow milk-white web nest between two rocks.

The thought of the operation became a nightmare. Every morning when I woke I imagined, Today they will seize me, shave my head, dope me, send me to the hospital in the city, and when I open my eyes I will have a bandage over my head and a scar at each temple or a curved one, like a halo, across the top of my head where the thieves, wearing gloves and with permission and delicacy, have entered and politely ransacked the storehouse and departed calm and unembarrassed like meter readers, furniture removers, or decorators sent to repaper an upstairs room.

And my "old" self? Having had warning of its approaching death will it have crept away like an animal to die in privacy? Or will it be spilled somewhere like an invisible stain? Or, discarded, will it lie in wait for me in the future, seeking revenge? What is the essence of it, that the thieves are like meter readers who unknowingly bear away a blank card, and furniture removers trustfully sweating at the weight of imaginary furniture?

I will wake and have no control over myself. I have seen others, how they wet the bed, how their faces are vague and loose with a supply of unreal smiles for which there is no real demand. I will be "retrained"—that is the word used for lobotomy cases. Rehabilitated. Fitted, my mind cut and tailored to the ways of the world. The nurses will take me for walks in the garden when I will wear a scarf over my head, with a butterfly bow at the top, as if I were hiding nothing more important than hair curlers, yet no one, least of all myself, will be fooled: it will be a lobotomy scarf—they have a supply of them—the joyous advertisement of changed personalities. And everyone will take an interest in me, talk to me, and for a time have patience with me as a working novelty like a miniature piano or a toy printing set where they may express or impress a small part of themselves until they are seized with the frustration that children feel when they are unable to transfer their entire selves to such limiting toys, or that adults feel when a child which they thought to be a toy becomes the dangerous reality of an individual being, as if the miniature piano had sounded forth symphonies.

Soon they will be irritated with me, exasperated; for much of living is an attempt to preserve oneself by annexing and occupying others. They will find that they cannot pour their ideas of my changed self into me like liquid into the waiting mold, for surely nothing will have changed the mold itself. Or will it be changed? What exactly will they have stolen—the gentle burglars busy at my brain? I knew there was no escape yet I cried Help Help, but I was buried in the wall until Dr. Portman heard me.

One Friday Dr. Portman came through the ward, and although I had never spoken to him since I said good-bye nine years ago when I was leaving Ward Four, I suddenly ran up to him and pulled at his sleeve, and in defiance of Matron's horrified gaze, I spoke to him.

"What is your opinion?" I asked.

He turned inquiringly to me. Patients did not usually interrupt his rounds and any delay in his progress caused as much concern among the staff as if an important train carrying bullion had been held up by bandits. As it was, he always hurried on his journey through the ward giving only an occasional nod of recognition like a train that does not stop at intermediate stations yet sometimes has a small flag hung out as a signal that it has passed by.

This day when I spoke to him he stopped in astonishment while Matron Glass, who herself was in awe of him, moved forward, policing the area surrounding him.

"What is my opinion?" he asked fiercely, adding in a more gentle tone, "What do you mean, Istina?"

Since I was concerned, day and night, with the operation on my brain, it seemed to me strange that other people were not continually thinking of it; for although the staff excitedly discussed my "future" (they reminded me of children wondering about their Christmas presents), they scarcely gave a thought to the operation itself, to its real meaning and the fact that, with the doctors' advice and

218

approval and my parents' consent, the self that for nearly thirty years had fought with time and, painstakingly, like a colony of ants bearing away the slain army, had carried the dead seconds, minutes, hours, over the difficult, slowly habitual tracks to the nest, the central storehouse—that self was to be assaulted, perhaps demolished.

"What do you mean, Istina?" Dr. Portman repeated.

"The lobotomy," I said, and felt dismay as the word escaped from me, for I was afraid of it and had kept it hidden, like a poisonous beetle shut in a matchbox.

Dr. Portman spoke instantly. "I say no," he said. "I don't want you changed. I want you to stay as you are."

I believed him and trusted him. He said it was not too late to cancel the preparations.

That night in my small room I wept and looked for Mr. Griffiths to tell him of my delight in my reprieve, but Mr. Griffiths did not visit me. Perhaps he found the room too cold and had gone to stay in the warmth of the mattress shed. It had pleased my sense of the melodramatic to know that, in the tradition of all prisoners condemned or reprieved, I had a mouse to confide in.

XIV

*S*OME DAYS AFTERWARDS Dr. Trace came
up to me in the park where I sat as peaceful and unconcerned
with time or new contents as an empty green medicine
bottle. The sight of Dr. Trace gave me a feeling of anticipation—had he brought the pictures to show me? In my
mind it seemed as if the pictures and my telling stories
about them would save me from all brain operations, even
from secret arousals and abductions in the night when Dr.
Portman was not there to rescue me. Yet I was shy, so
great was my reliance upon the pictures that I did not like
to talk of them, as one hesitates to mention in public the
name of someone secretly loved. I waited for Dr. Trace to
speak.

"You shouldn't be in this ward," he said. "We're going
to give you insulin treatment. And after that, we'll see."

He said nothing about the pictures and I began to feel
afraid for I remembered that insulin treatment was given
to people to prepare them for lobotomy, to fatten them up,
as it were, for the kill; and they had said that I was too
thin—too thin for what? Were they planning to operate
suddenly, without warning, so that one day, upon waking,

I should go to the door of myself and find the bailiffs entering as if by right to remove my furniture, and I should not be able to stop them?

"Remember," Dr. Trace added as he went toward the park gate, "I'm going to show you some pictures."

I smiled then. Ah, I thought, between Dr. Trace and me, that is our secret.

Another day I was sitting in the park thinking about the pictures and imagining the thousand and one stories I would tell to save my conscience and my dreams from being chopped off, when the nurse came to fetch me.

"You're going to Ward Four," she said. "You and Susan."

So we returned to Ward Four and were taken to the dayroom and told to sit near the fire, and people made room for us on the long leather sofa because they said we looked cold.

"Why do you look so frightened?" they asked me.

I did not realize that I had acquired a permanent attitude of fear. I cringed from people when they spoke to me and tried to hide in the corner when Sister Honey came into the room. Her stern expression frightened me. Everything frightened me. I kept shivering as if I had been out all night without shelter or clothes.

"We won't eat you," Sister Honey said in her kindest voice. "Sit down by the fire and get warm and talk to the other patients."

It was strange to be amongst people who talked, and at first I could not grasp the idea of talking, making sentences aloud, entering conversation, shunting back and forth with words in the once-darkened carriages lit with meaning. And where were the Ward Two people, where was Edith to take my arm and say, "Now never you mind and don't be afraid; Edith will look after you."

These people of Ward Four seemed so confident and powerful and full of plans and clear as hawks, and for a moment I wanted to be back with Maudie and Carol and Dame Mary-Margaret and Hilary and Brenda who did not stare in surprise if you chose not to answer their questions or if you said something strange. In Ward Two nobody was surprised at another's behavior or speech or silence— for these were people's natural rights, like the customs of foreign lands. But here the patients seemed to be judging, to be exercising the civilized horror pain delight that form a protective crust over the deeper surgings of individual feeling. And they talked of the future as if it were something tangible and within reach, like a ripe pear hanging over the fence from a neighbor's garden, whereas I had known for so long now that the future had been attacked by worms that had crept into it and eaten its heart. Faith might be a good neighbor and hang fruit over the fence but something else was needed to wield the arsenic spray.

After a while I came from the corner of the dayroom and warmed my hands by the fire. I was grateful for the fire. And now I was glad to be in Ward Four with Mrs. Pilling and Mrs. Everett coming for volunteers to set the tables, and still she was worrying about everything, about the silver, and the sugar basins being filled, and the eggs being boiled for the observation dormitory. And once or twice Mrs. Pilling entered with a grave careful expression to consult the nurse on important domestic matters such as should we have marmalade when so much is left over or jam when the tin is nearly empty?

"Which ward are you from?" the patients asked me.

It seemed a personal question like scent age income dreams revenge. I smiled secretively. Brick Building Ladies, Lavatory Ladies, Park Ladies, Yard Ladies—not any more, and only Lavatory Ladies before treatment, before E.S.T., and I was not having E.S.T.

I burst out laughing, and one of the patients sitting by the fire said to another, "Look, she's laughing."

My bed was in the observation dormitory where I had first slept nine years ago, and although I was afraid at the sight of the treatment room at the end, I felt safe enough, for my treatment was going to be insulin and I reasoned that if somebody kills you by poisoning, another is scarcely likely to try and shoot you. But Susan and I became ill, and were put to bed, side by side, and for many days I lay in bed watching the others getting up and working and preparing for treatment; and when Matron Glass came through on her rounds I cowered under the bedclothes, for she looked at me as a gardener looks at a weed that has sprung up in the middle of a fine flower bed.

"What are you doing here?" she asked on my first day in bed.

Sister Honey told her, and smiled at me, and said, "We're wheeling you out on the veranda in the sun."

So day after day I watched the nurses going to and from the Nurses' Home, and the patients pegging their washing on the rope clothesline strung between the poplars, and it was their own clothes, not stout striped flannel pants and thick ward socks and scarecrow nighties; and the workers returning from the Home with the leftovers—dried apricots, squares of jam tart—to be put on the table in the middle of the dining room, as extras for tea; and the pig-boy and the coal lorries passing, and the man with the rubber plunger to clear the blocked drains, and Dr. Portman's son riding his new bicycle along the gravel path; and I looked at the flowers in the garden, the granny's bonnets and dusty millers and marigolds and it seemed that the shredded strong scent of the marigolds reached my nose. Someone gave me a magazine; idly I turned the pages, not caring about the voluptuous jellies and the spawn of rainbow cakes with their white sugary secretion lying upon the oven tray.

Susan was in the bed beside me. She never spoke. At times she smiled and looked puzzled; at other times she coughed. I turned from her because she reminded me of Ward Two, and seemed to have been set beside me, like a memory which I had barred from my mind yet which was determined, even if it had to present itself in human shape, to be my lifelong guest.

But I felt overcome with sadness and guilt when I saw the Ward Two patients being brought in the mornings for treatment, hopping and skipping and held by the nurses and wearing the familiar red flannel dressing gowns and gray ward socks. Yet they were not strange people to me, for I knew them and could communicate with them, and it seemed that by leaving Ward Two I had betrayed them. When they saw me and recognized me and spoke to me I felt a wild delight and reverence as if a voice had spoken to me from a cloud.

Bertha was there one morning with three nurses.

"Hello," I said shyly.

"Hello upon my word," she exclaimed. "I'm going for the shock treatment." Then she began to struggle and the nurses closed in on her and dragged her into the dormitory.

Some days later Susan and I went to the city for an X ray, and Susan was found to have tuberculosis, and was put in one of the small rooms down the corridor next to Margaret and to Eva who woke one morning, vomited, and died, and her mother, a small woman with bandy legs and wearing a gray coat, came to collect her things.

XV

"*R*EADY FOR INSULIN?" they said.

After the early morning injection three other patients and myself were put to bed in the "Wire" dormitory, a room that resembled a chicken coop or an aviary, for the top half of two of the walls was made of wire netting; also, as there was little ventilation from the one small window, in the early morning after having been filled with sleeping people the room had the distinct odor of a farmyard. We sat, propped by pillows, and were instructed to keep awake by talking and sewing or knitting until slowly we were overtaken by a double vision and confusion.

Always, then, I entered a region of snow and ice, and my mother's face, like that of a witch with her nose meeting her chin, warned me never to sleep in the snow—that it is the easiest desire to give way to. Never sleep in the snow! Therefore I struggled through the drifts with my shoes clogged, and my clothes and the hollows of my flesh like earth pockets and valleys filled with snow; and the brilliant whiteness increased until it could no longer bear its own intensity, when it changed suddenly to deadly black velvet, like love which overstrains itself into hate, or like the dark side of our nature which we meet most suddenly when we believe ourselves to be journeying farthest from it.

The heaviness of the snow divided, becoming small flakes like flying needles or claws of tiny white birds digging my cheeks. I was awake and glucose was being poured in a tube down my throat.

We would have breakfast then and go with the nurse to the occupational-therapy department which had been opened in the renovated veranda facing the tennis courts, down near the front of the hospital. The room was filled with sun from the east and the sea lay marbled blue, stabbed with light. I sat and absorbed the warmth that was pale gold like the reeds that people were twisting and plaiting to make baskets and cradles. Others were weaving scarves in bright colors on small hand looms or lengths of material on larger looms whose framework seemed complicated like a meccano set with all the pieces in use. Others made soft felt toys—ducks, rabbits, bears, all supposedly complimented by being given human expressions and dressed in hats and coats and aprons.

"What do you want to make?" asked the occupational therapist, a young woman in a yellow overall. She had just been giving the patients morning tea and was guarding the biscuit tin to prevent second helpings. "Do you want to make a scarf, a basket? A toy? Cross stitch on tapestry? A cushion cover?"

I didn't want to make anything. I wanted to sit and watch the sunlight and the shadows of the people moving in and out of the open door, and the skeins of light weaving themselves into the warm colors of the materials at the looms.

"I can't think what I want to make," I said.

227

So the occupational therapist gave me a wooden base and some reeds which had been soaked in a bucket of water, and I think I should have felt very sad just sitting there twisting reeds in and out of other reeds, had not the toothpaste arrived, a kerosene tin of it, and boxes of tubes, and the task was to fill the tubes with toothpaste, government toothpaste suitably gray with a consistency that reminded me of cake mixture made with sea-gull droppings.

So I filled the tubes, rolling the ends to seal them, and I was thankful that even if the secret of tomorrow, of the people of Ward Two, of my own fears and distortions, were hidden from me, at least I surely knew something that would help me to "take my place in the world"—I knew how toothpaste came to be put in tubes!

Sometimes with the other three insulin patients I played tennis on the court outside the veranda, and once I saw Dr. Steward looking from the window of his office, and I thought: He is looking at me and thinking why did he not transfer me sooner from Ward Two; he is thinking that perhaps there are others in Ward Two for whom all hope has been abandoned and the preparations made to "change the personality," to "reduce the tension," yet who still may be helped without their brain being ravaged and the most powerful trees felled that grow in the forest.

After some weeks when the treatment was finished and the staff's personal attention (and the supply of golden barley sugar) suddenly withdrawn, like the sun going down, the four of us—Nola, Madge, Eve and myself—returned once more to our separate darkness—like rabbits returning to their burrows after a sunny day among the turnips. We seemed happier and fatter. Nola went home to her husband and new baby. Madge, who was found to have tuberculosis, was put in a small room down the corridor next to Susan. Eve, whose home was in the North Island, packed her many suitcases of fashionable clothing and was farewelled by Dr. Portman himself who showed a wisely provincial respect for "foreigners" whether they lived miles away over seas and mountains and plains or dreams away in a comparable distance of the mind.

And I was transferred to the "Wire" dormitory where I knew the "chronic" cases slept—those who would eventually go to Ward One or, if they became violent and uncooperative, to Ward Two. And once again I heard the groaning and grinding of ice that surrounded me and I glimpsed the faces of people embedded in the ice and staring at me with a rigid bloodless gaze.

Icebergs in a hencoop you ask? Yes, and glaciers and hailstones and snow and a glistening border of snails and the sun cracking the wheat.

I shuddered when they said "The Wire Dormitory. You're being moved to the Wire Dormitory." And I smelled through the ice a cage of ferrets balanced between turkeys and bantams in a dark corner of the guard's van at the end of a slow train traveling on rusty rails through a wilderness of dried river beds littered with the gray splintered skulls of sheep and cattle; I smelled a farmyard and death and hawks and river stones and old branches of trees hung with snag skirts of rushes and snowgrass.

And I smelled the dead horse that nobody owned; they came and stared at it and prodded its blown belly and its face where decay and the flies had settled first like kisses

229

on its mouth; and they went away and wrote letters to the council and the newspaper and a man came in the night and buried it, but nobody ever claimed it, for death is no one's possession.

The smells froze in the ice and vanished and the two travelers came walking in step in black hoods and tennis shoes and the clouds, like packs of snow, were shuffled in the sky and dealt with their faces to the sun.

I slept in the corner bed. Josie slept next to me. She was a tall dark woman who walked up and down singing "A-pompy a-pompy a-pompy" and who, during the war, had met and married one of the American Marines who had promised, when he returned to the United States, to "send for her." Opposite me slept Doris a tiny woman who needed to be helped into bed, it was so high for her to climb, and one had to be so careful not to stare at her.

"I might do, in a dollhouse," she would say bitterly. Her sewing was the neatest I have seen, like that of the legendary small people who climb at night into the flowers and embroider the petals or sit on stalks of grass knitting dewdrops, or the evil folk who creep in people's eyes and draw the curtains and furtively stitch tapestries with poisoned needle and thread or have their workroom in people's ears, tatting back and forth with their shuttle full of decibels. Time and again, with Doris and other dwarves and patients who resembled witches or seemed inhabited by dragons, one felt like a witness to the origins of folklore; one felt that such people, whose only home in the world was a mental hospital, would have their problem solved if they could indeed dwell in the cups of flowers or behind people's eyes, or in cottages deep in the wood with poisonous thorns in the garden and a one-eyed cat waiting at the front door.

I was still afraid at mealtimes. I sat next to Miss Wallace a gentle silver-haired woman who had been a music mistress and was inclined sometimes to talk to us as if we had not practiced our scales. But she was usually depressed and in the morning her eyes were always red with weeping, for she was troubled at night by radar in her room, and no one, neither her relatives nor the hospital staff, would believe her.

They kept saying it was her imagination, her illness.

Sleeping in the Wire Dormitory, which was really a ward lumber room for oddities and castoffs, I plunged again into depression and hopelessness. Wherever I went the smell of human compost seemed to follow me and distinguish me and the others of the Wire Dormitory from the rest of the ward. I felt the shame of being locked in at night when the people of the two lower dormitories were allowed to come and go as they pleased, to make themselves a milk drink on the fire and help themselves from the plate of leftover bread and butter which Mrs. Pilling put out on the sideboard, and to sit in the dayroom with the door open, knitting, talking, or listening to the radio until nine o'clock. My weeks of treatment seemed without purpose if I were to continue the dreary routine among the condemned. Sometimes, at night, if I closed my eyes and smelled and listened, I could believe that I was back in Treecroft, in Four-Five-and-One.

They began to threaten me at night and scream in my ear

and their faces bulged in close-ups. Their eyes were made of mercury.

"She'll end up in Ward Two," they said.

Until one morning Dr. Steward asked to see me.

"I wonder if you would make morning and afternoon tea for the doctors?"

"Oh" I said. "Oh."

"I've given you full parole, and I want you to come tomorrow morning to the room off the dispensary where we have our tea. The occupational therapist will show you what to do. Get away from the ward for a change, eh?"

Then looking about him and speaking distinctly as if to make sure that any witnesses could repeat his words at a future trial, he added, disclaiming responsibility, his pale face grave, "This is Dr. Trace's idea. He trusts you."

There was always talk of trust, with the doctor inquiring as if his life depended upon it, "Do you trust me, will you trust me," and expecting you to say eagerly and without reservation, "Yes, yes," when you knew, privately, that he scarcely had time to trust himself in the confusion and tiredness that accompanied the day-and-night attempt to solve the human division sum that had been omitted from his mathematical training: If one thousand women depend upon one and a half doctors how much time must be devoted to each patient in one year; state the answer in minutes, and with eggs at three shillings a dozen, and allowing three minutes for each egg boiled consecutively, what is your change out of five shillings? Enough to buy a cup of coffee.

"Dr. Trace trusts you," Dr. Steward repeated.

Remembering Dr. Trace and the pictures, and the stories

I had planned to tell to save myself, I felt the longing that comes when the hovering dead finally withdraw themselves and return unopened all communications addressed to them. If only Dr. Trace had shown me the pictures that day in the park!

On my first morning at work I felt so proud, collecting the keys from the hook inside Dr. Steward's office and resisting the temptation to explore the files, visiting the stores for butter and jam and going behind the counter to choose the jam, fetching the scones and bread from the big kitchen, standing alone in the small room watching the clock, melting the butter, and hastily spreading crustless triangular sandwiches made with new warm bread. At ten o'clock the Zip heater began to scream and I made the tea. And there was Dr. Trace, smaller than I had remembered him but with his head still thrust on one side. Looking at his honest tired face I had the idea that he was wearing carpet slippers but no, they were polished brown shoes; and I expected him suddenly to walk up and down between rows of potatoes.

Of course. He was my grandfather, and his skin was stretched over his brow as if whatever lay inside his head had been packed tightly after first having been dried in the sun and stripped of unnecessary stalks and dead leaves. The lower half of his face was puckered, his mouth turned down as if he were going to cry, and the honesty in his face was that of age which has the same expression, sleeping and waking, and not of youth whose power and pride change to helpless innocence the moment it falls asleep.

He smiled at me. He was my grandfather and no doubt his pockets were full of striped mint lollies.

"You're making tea," he said.

Then I remembered the pictures and waited for him to mention them but he said nothing, and every second he began to look older and older and I thought perhaps he will die here drinking his tea and never show me the pictures.

Dr. Steward entered. He looked alarmed when he saw me, and then smiled, and he seemed to be secretly wondering if he had "done the right thing" by letting me come down to the front of the building, and giving me full parole.

More people came in. I had to stay to attend to the tea, and I stood by the window facing the sink, rinsing cups, and listening to the conversation of the Gods whom I had heard say only Good Morning, How are you today, You're looking well, It takes time you know, The tension will be reduced.

The tension will be reduced.

They talked to one another as if they were human, but their conversation fell strangely upon my ears, as if the mammoths in the Museum had begun to speak.

I still had the habit, more common in those who had been in hospital a long time, of investing the doctors' every remark and movement and their families and their possessions with a wonderful significance, and I stood there confused by the very fact of their speech and listening intently for prophecies and marvels.

Dr. Steward was speaking. "I can never keep a box of chocolates in the house. My wife has to hide them from me or I eat them all at once."

A commonplace remark, you will say. But I caught it and treasured it although it was not meant for me but was one of the clues that people drop, like Hansel and Gretel drop-

234

ping crumbs, to find their way out of the wild woods of themselves. But like the little birds I ate the crumbs not intended for me.

The doctors talked about cricket, pay increases, lists and schedules, interesting current cases in court, and no one except Dr. Portman dreamed that I was listening.

"Istina, would you mind leaving the room while we talk?"

Dr. Portman asked in a tone that showed he was giving orders. He was standing with his back to the fire, taking everybody's share of the fire. His black hair which had not been given enough morning oil stuck up like a rooster's comb. He poured some tea into his saucer and stooped to give it to his dog Molly who shared his walks and his rounds and his food and the front seat of his car.

I left the room. And from that day it was understood that I did not remain at the sink listening to the Gods in conversation.

Conversation is the wall we build between ourselves and other people, too often with tired words like used and broken bottles which, catching the sunlight as they lie embedded in the wall, are mistaken for jewels.

Sometimes I imagined that Dr. Trace came to me and said, "Now Istina, here are the pictures. Now you tell me the stories."

And I imagined it so often, with the pictures immense in my mind and the stories attached to them that I felt the irritation of being aroused from my dream world when one day Dr. Trace said, "Remember, I was going to show you some pictures?"

Granddad Trace, I thought, leaning over the potato

flowers with the back of his pants baggy and shiny and his eyes blue as the rim of the best teacup. Then I knew it was Dr. Trace telling me he would show me some pictures and asking if I remembered.

My heart beat fast with excitement as the stories began in my mind as if a switch had been turned to start the flow.

"Yes," I said. "I remember."

He shut the book he had been reading in the dinner hour. It was called *Boswell on the Grand Tour*.

"Well," he said. "There's no time. There won't be any pictures. It would take too long. And there's no time."

XVI

*I*N THE CORNER of Ward Four dayroom there was a glass cabinet which contained not cocktail glasses or china or fossils or labeled seaweeds on a bed of green plush, but three resident books on the top shelf with the lower shelf reserved for the floating population which the chaplain brought each month from the hospital library. The three books, unread as far as I could see, were *Girl of the Limberlost*, *Moths of the Limberlost* (I remember my mother once describing it as "a lovely book"), and a dusty volume *From Log Cabin to White House* with a frontispiece depicting the noble future President Garfield after a fight with one of his school fellows.

"Extending his hand in the magnanimous spirit of a victor he said, 'Murphy, give us your hand.'"

Sometimes a patient would wander over to the cabinet, draw out one of the books, flip the pages quickly like a cardsharp getting ready to deal, then close the book and return it to the shelf. When the chaplain came he brought books with big print and pictures where the characters were children or young adults who did wrong and were punished and made to see the evil of their ways, or who did good and died and went to heaven. The good characters, like the heroes with their white hats and white horses in the cowboy films, could be identified by their golden hair.

Most of these books were old Sunday School prizes contributed by people in the village and were gold-embossed inside the cover with inscriptions (where angels peeped from entwined honeysuckle or clematis) which read "Awarded to Lily Stevens for Good Conduct" or "Tom Robson for good work in Class Four." The date was usually the end of the nineteenth century or the beginning of the twentieth, for in spite of the gradual adoption of the "new" attitude, the idea still prevailed that mental illness was a form of childish naughtiness which might be cured in a Victorian environment with the persuasion of stern speech and edifying literature. And although the library was new, with a growing range of books, the chaplain persisted in bringing us these Sunday School prizes that might do us "good," and teach us the evil of our ways. And there was another reason for his choice of old books; he did not trust us to care for the bright new volumes. He believed, with most other people, that mental patients are destructive by nature, and if he had had his choice I think he would have given us the cloth and wooden books that one gives to infants as one gives a dog bones to worry.

Every three months the van from the Country Library Service called at the hospital and left about sixty books of all classifications which were chosen by the chaplain or members of the office staff or perhaps the doctors or occupational therapists, but rarely by nurses or attendants who were regarded in the hierarchy as belonging to the lowest social scale.

238

Now one day I was standing washing or drying teacups and looking out of the window on to the front lawn when the van from the library service drew up outside and the librarian got out and opened the doors at the back and there, almost within my reach, were shelves packed with books dazzling lurid sober stiff covered, slim volumes of art prints, heavy sagas of the deep South.

I felt the excitement tinged with gloom and foreboding that I first experienced when I was ten and joined the town library (called formidably Athenaeum and Mechanics Institute) and could not get in without passing the wicked-looking stuffed moa standing at the foot of the stairs, and a sharp-tongued librarian who sat behind a grille dispensing tickets and fines and books and keeping her eye on the adjoining Reading Room where the old men sat, petrified by the SILENCE notices.

It seemed to me that books must be wonderful treasures if they were to be reached only at the end of such a forbidding journey, and that books were only for brave people who were not afraid of giant stuffed birds with glass eyes.

And the fact that there were notices demanding Silence when one would never have dreamed of speaking made it seem,that the room contained secret presences which had to be controlled and which related in a strange way the death and painstaking reconstruction of the moa and the micelike letters that were wired with meaning and resurrected to make words, and placed in imposing attitudes on the pages of the books. So it was for her own protection that the librarian hid behind a grille and pinned notices on the wall; she had to make every effort to subdue more than the timid subscribers tiptoeing between the shelves.

After so many years in hospital, the sight of so many books made me forget that one has to be a fearless pilgrim to arrive safely at a library. I went out and spoke to the librarian. "May I go inside and look at the books?"

She smiled. "Certainly."

I walked up the ramp and stood in the van, trying to decide where to begin my inspection of the concealed words whose bones were molded together by men to make either an awesome vision of truth that would guard any door of the mind, or a creature that would stand for a while, deceptively whole, then collapse, scattering across the threshold the dry dead bones that did not even burst into flame at their friction one with the other.

I was standing gazing and dreaming when suddenly the chaplain appeared in the doorway of the van. He knew me. He had seen me in Ward Two, in the park and the yard. He spread his hands in a quick movement, as if to bear the precious books safely to him.

"Come out of there," he said sharply to me.

"Oh please let me look at them. I won't touch any. I promise."

The chaplain looked more horrified.

"No patient is allowed in there. No patient is allowed in the van. Come out this instant."

He looked about him as if searching for someone to "deal" with me in the way that, he knew, mental patients are dealt with if they become obstinate.

I walked out of the van. After the excitement of seeing the books and then being denied a chance to look at them by someone who, curiously lacking in understanding for a chaplain, had said, making the old distinction between patients and people, "No patient is allowed," I was almost in tears.

There I had been standing, drearily drying cups and thinking perhaps about dinner or mail or the Wire Dormitory where I still spent the night, when suddenly a library had appeared just outside the window and a tweedy fairy godmother had not denied my request to look inside. But the villain arrived and turned me away because I had not the status necessary for people who view shelves of books. I was a patient and could not be trusted; I was a child and would not grasp the content, the essential meaning, of the books.

He sees the land of meaning, and one path to it, and the so-called "normal" people traveling swiftly and in comfort to the land; he does not include the shipwrecked people who arrive by devious lonely routes, and the many who dwell in the land in the beginning.

I returned to the tearoom and put away the last cups, hung the tea towel to dry, switched off the Zip heater, replaced the keys, carefully observing the routine in a melodramatic way as if someone had died and I had announced heroically that I would "keep going." I tried not to cry.

The chaplain had spoken to me as if I suffered from a disease that would infect the books. Was he right? I returned to the ward and went to the dayroom and stayed surveying the usual dismal scene, the lonely muddled old ladies and the bewildered new patients trying to get used to the idea of being in Cliffhaven and being locked up and the fires being locked and the windows opening only six inches and the nurses commanding Dayroom Ladies, Bed Ladies, Rise Ladies.

Then a nurse called me, "Sister wants you."

What had I done? Was I being transferred to Ward Two? Were they taking me away to shave my head for an operation, in spite of Dr. Portman?

"Sister wants you. Hurry."

Sister Honey was standing behind the serving table setting the roast on its board ready for the matron to carve. She told me that Dr. Portman had rung up and wanted me to go immediately to his office.

So Dr. Portman had changed his mind, he had decided they would bore two holes in the side of my head for my unsuitable personality to fly out like a migrating bird to another country and never return not even when spring came and the cherry blossom opened and the spindly wild plum showed white along the paddock fences.

I was afraid and went alone down to the front of the hospital and was standing in the wide polished hall being gazed at by the heavily featured brown and maroon portraits of past administrators and philanthropists and village councilors when Dr. Portman came in the front door and hurried towards me. He was excited; his cheeks were flecked with red.

"Come out to the library van, Istina," he urged.

We went to the van. He walked up the ramp and beckoned me to follow. I entered royally. And then he explained that about sixty books had to be chosen for the hospital library and would I kindly help to choose them?

There was no sign of the chaplain. I wonder what he, the villain, would have said if he had seen me entertained by the tubby loud-voiced intelligent intuitive prince in the forbidden castle.

Both formality and dinner forgotten we sat on the floor

of the little library, choosing. Sometimes Dr. Portman read passages aloud and turned his own memories with their dark side to face the light. And it was late afternoon when, with a headache of happiness, I returned to the ward. And from that day I felt in myself a reserve of warmth from which I could help myself, like coal from the cellar on a winter's day, if the snow came or if the frost fell in the night to blacken the flowers and wither the new fruit.

I began to go out walking more often by myself and once I went down to the village store which was not out of bounds and bought myself—a jar of peanut butter. And often I remembered the patients of Ward Two, and on my way to the canteen I passed the dirty dayroom and the clean dayroom, and Brenda in her striped dress tottered to the window to say hello.

"Hello Miss Istina Mavet." She pouted and then smiled. If she were in the clean dayroom she would play a piece of music for me, if Mr. Frederick Barnes allowed her. And Carol would squat down by the window and tell me the latest news of her "gagement" and the further details she had worked out for the wedding which was not after all to be with the pig-boy or with any of Hilary's friends, but with a stranger. "Some enchanted evening you may see a stranger."

"Strangers are best," said Carol. "Best for marrying. Strangers or film stars. And I'm 'clined for the man on the radio—Roy."

Roy was the announcer who controlled the Sunday request programs patronized by Hilary and Carol; their latest favorite was still

> On top of old Smoky all covered in snow
> I lost my true lover through courting so slow

where once again life seemed to depend on a swifter warmth than most people, even lovers, are prepared to give; one can only assume that the loved one lies frozen to death on the top of Old Smoky. While I would be talking to Carol, Maudie liked to come to the window to have her say, for one of her duties as God was that of a commentator on the affairs of Ward Two.

"Istina Mavet is standing by the window. Istina Mavet is talking to Carol. Down you go, Istina Mavet."

Looking through the window I felt depressed and hopeless at the sameness of everything. Living is so much like one of those childhood games where you keep shutting your eyes and on opening them expect to find everything changed—a new city with glass towers, a table laden for a feast, a kindly forest where the trees no longer strike blows or twist themselves into fearful shapes.

In Ward Two it was still the same. First tea, Ladies. Lavatory Ladies, Bed Ladies. Bed. And the rushing under the cut-out daisy stars and the cold sky to the cheerless Brick Building and the urine-saturated floors and straw-smelling rooms; and the long evening and night.

Cannot one exercise one's will as a living hammer to force the shape of change?

I could not stop thinking of the people of Ward Two— Brenda, Zoe, Mona, Maudie, the total alienation of Esme, her sitting alone in a puddled corner, her striped dress over her head, no pants on, her feet bare, her black eyes gleaming in her pale face through the slits in the front of her dress; the animal cries, the bird speech. And the hidden people of Ward One—the children, the old ladies, the idiots, the withered yet ageless mongols with their dumpy bodies and their faithful ways, their neat trotting to and fro on simple errands, their absorbed gazing at what they and others will never comprehend. And then the patients who, when they are undressed at night, are found to have their fingers clenched tightly over something which they refuse to surrender, as if they said, You can have the blue striped dress, and the flannelette pants, bunchy, reaching to the knee, and the gray woolen ward stockings, and the v-necked striped garment known in official records as a *chemise*, but these you cannot have—the stalks of grass which I picked for myself in the park, the piece of silver paper from somebody's chocolate, the ball of hair that I found on the floor of the bathroom; my treasures that give meaning to my long day of sitting crouched, hands over my knees, staring from the yellowed patch of park grass to the sun in the sky, Lord Landless in the King's White Hall.

XVII

"*IF IT KEEPS FINE,*" the nurse said, "they'll open the bowling green tomorrow."

It was a late October twilight. I was sitting on the window seat in the dayroom looking down at the masses of trees that were beginning to give shelter to the homeless dark just arriving and stowing its black stick and bundle by walls and leaves, in corners and hollows; the light stayed on the lawn and in the lower spaces of sky, and hallucinated thrushes kept hopping about or standing, head on one side, listening to the secret voices. Swift blackbirds in a take-off twitter of excitement flew low from tree to tree or dived in the earth where the pink middle-aged worms wearing their body belts sat knitting by their fire of decay and wondering if rain would come in the night and they would be flooded from their home and drowned.

I was absorbed and staring and half-heard what the nurse had said. The bowling green? But I was going home soon and primitive ceremonies did not interest me. That day, after I had served Dr. Steward with his morning tea and scone and jam I had said, "When will I be allowed to go home?" and he had answered, "I think anytime now, if anyone is willing to have you."

I ignored the implication of his conditional clause and told him that certainly my people would "have me." Who are we, have we changed when we no longer claim as our treasure the stalk of grass in our hand or the chocolate paper but choose the human beings that we hope to hold tight in our heart? Are we sane then? Have we progressed from illness when we do not care any more for the pink cretonne bag with its pattern of roses, but begin to look for people that we may thread a drawstring round their neck and carry them back and forth inside ourselves, and not be willing to let them go not even in the night in sleep and dreams? Yes, I knew that my family would "have me," although I knew that they were strangers now, that my mother was a bird and my father was a sandstone image, and the whole world was a dream world where people wake and work and love and sleep, free, ebullient as Yo-yos until the cord retrieves them again and again to the central prison of their perplexity. In the darkness of their gaudily striped fairground of days their hearts grow cold with fright as they see the sinister conjurer loosening the chains which they desire always to bind them to themselves. For they are separate and cannot escape from their restraining selves like a child who wants to play hide-and-go-seek but who dares not ever leave the "den" for fear he is trapped and revealed to himself and others as "he"—the culprit, the criminal.

What shall I do, I thought, if I go home? I cannot live my life escaping into pine plantations and gossiping with morning-tea magpies in a bargain basement of fine feathers and fearing that the tide of blood will rise in my mother's shoes that sit like empty cradles in the wardrobe and that my father will graze his sandstone eyes on tomorrow and go blind or bruise the time itself into darkness.

I thought Shall I be a cloud?

Yes my people will have me and the world will receive me with open arms like one of those iron-spiked creatures in the horror films that embrace their victims to death.

"You are dreaming," the nurse said. "I was talking about the bowling green."

The opening of the bowling green was one of the hospital occasions and was held each year in early summer at the men's bowling green on the hill and was accompanied by the usual feast of sandwiches and cakes and fizz. There was little excitement in Ward Four when the nurse gave the news, but when I passed through the corridor later that evening to look in at Susan and say hello, I saw Mrs. Pilling in her room carefully hanging her best dress over the chair. She looked guilty when she saw me and hastily shut the door. She knew that no matter how unperturbed the other patients might be, for the people who would be in hospital until they died the opening of the bowling green was a true festival. And I saw Mrs. Everett removing the two old flatirons from the dining room fire and cleaning the soot from them; and she went to bed early and did not stay to help with the hot milk drinks; only she and Mrs. Pilling were really excited, and seemed to be telling themselves, like parents warning their children: Now early to bed with you, there's a long tiring day ahead.

Yet the ceremony took only half an hour.

It was a cold day with a gray wadding of cloud, and a chilly wind blowing from the sea, and we climbed in a small disdainful group up the hill beyond the men's ward, and pushed through the battered wooden turnstile to the bowling green with its windbreak of young firs hushing and sighing and its small pavilion with the adjoining room where the gear was kept and where the feast waited to be distributed. The panorama was of hospital towers and trees and sea and misted horizon. Above the green, to the right, we could see the new ward for chronic women patients; its buildings were painted a bright yellow, supposed to give a feeling of happiness yet seeming to bring only further depression to those who had outlived the severity of their illness and the interest of their relatives and were now to spend their lives in a home where tranquility, by prescription, was put in the pastel-shaded walls, and happiness painted on the roof, as a sad and reminding second best to the redecoration that could not be made in human minds and hearts. We stood beside the bowling green, waiting. I remembered at once, with a shudder, that beyond the sour dark bush trees—leatherleaf, cabbage trees, and the twisted fence posts, and the swampy paddock where the cows stood after milking, swishing their tails and chewing their cud, someone years ago now had shown me the slaughterhouse with its concrete floors and dilapidated pens, and said grimly, "They kill on Wednesdays."

It was Miss Caddick who told me. She died under E.S.T. because she was not wearing long woolen stockings. "That's the slaughterhouse," she said. And then, pointing to an old building with the paint peeling from its walls, she looked mysteriously about her and whispered, "That's Simla."

Simla?

The lawn was smooth and green, an imitation. I was afraid.

I watched the eager little group from Ward Two with their floppy felt hats and party dresses, come straggling through the turnstile, Carol ahead with Hilary, Brenda advancing slowly and cautiously with no wall to support her, Maudie in the coat that was too small for her majestic figure, Minnie Cleave, Mrs. Shaw, one or two patients from the dirty day-room; and aloof, and wearing her celebration head scarf, Dame Mary-Margaret who rarely took part in festivals.

One of the men patients, like a wax model in a shop window, stood grasping a roller; he was the only person on the green and he did not move; he was like one of the people in the fairy story who were under a spell and stuck to whatever they touched. Others on the edge of the green where the grass sprang uncurbed were practicing bowling, taking care that the bowl did not approach the green; and among these was Eric in long white tennis shoes that had no laces, and a white panama hat over his bald head. He was explaining, teaching, demonstrating; he evidently knew the secret of playing bowls just as he knew the secret of dancing and giving out prizes in tents and producing silk handkerchiefs from a top hat. I have never met a man who knew so many secrets; but although he behaved as if he had opened all the lucky packets of life he never disclosed what he really found in them and one suspects that it was only trinkets that broke when he touched them.

But would Dr. Portman never arrive; for without him there was no ceremony and no feast? Now there was Dr. Steward without his wife but shouldering his little boy and being stared at in wonder and admiration by the woman patients, especially those of Ward Two, who could not keep their eyes off him, gaping at the marvel of him, see, standing there with his son, smiling and talking and seeming human, and wearing ordinary clothes and not a white coat but a heavy tweed overcoat against the chilly breeze. He felt the cold, you see, like other people. Look, he was turning up his collar and drawing into the shelter of the slight fire, and the sea breeze did not know he was a doctor but was blowing his hair and nipping his ears and his nose; how could it have dared?

I saw the spellbound gaze of the Ward Two patients and I recoiled from the facts of illness and hospitals that make the comings and goings of an ordinary human being seem like prodigious events: I recoiled because I envied, knowing the few human conditions—love, starvation, imminent death—which construe as miracle the hieroglyphic commonplace. And yet I recoiled because I knew it was not love or imminent death which made the patients gaze at Dr. Steward and his child; it was a kind of starvation that is not relieved by rainbow cake or Sports Day fizz.

The Superintendent arrived in sports clothes, his wife in her leopard-skin coat, walking beside him, his red setter Molly, trotting behind. Dr. Portman walked majestically, confidently. After a few words with the attendants he stepped to the green, testing it with his smart suede shoes, then withdrawing them quickly, for he knew that desecration would be allowed only after he had given the word and bowled the first bowl of the season. Clearing his throat he spoke the customary words which came easily to him, as conventional phrases are often the secret delight of unconventional people who use them as vehicles to get from here to there and not as temples or dwelling places.

"It gives me great pleasure. No doubt you who are gathered here today . . . I know you are all eagerly waiting to partake of the refreshments . . . this auspicious occasion . . ."

An attendant handed Dr. Portman a polished bowl; he adjusted the bias, stooped to the green, guided the bowl forward and declared the season open, to applause which came mostly from the patients of Ward Two who understood the solemnity of the rites. The rest of the spectators went towards the pavilion where attendants began to hand out sandwiches and cakes and fizz, while the officials retired to the small room for their special feast of cream cakes and ham sandwiches. We ate our share, the paste and pickle sandwiches and the puffed-up hollow cakes and the plain golden-hearted currantless cakes, and the melon tarts, and while some of us complained that "those in the room" were getting the best of the feast, there were no complaints from the patients of Ward Two who again understood the rites, and would have been dismayed and confused (at first) to be given fancy cakes.

Now one by one the patients who had parole and those from the convalescent ward began to move away making remarks like "What was all the fuss about?" "You would have thought something marvelous was going to happen, and it was only Dr. Portman, the show-off, bowling the first bowl and what is there in that?"

These patients appeared dignified and bored; after the opening speech they had clapped lightly; they had not rushed forward in a starving mob when they saw the sandwiches and cakes appearing; some had even declined the bottle of fizz which was theirs *by right*. But there, in one corner of the pavilion, Carol was exuberantly setting up a fizz exchange, a green for those who didn't like the red, an orange for those who had been given a lemon drink. And now on the green the men were walking about testing the surface bowling the bowls; the atmosphere was relaxed; the crowd was leaving. Soon there was no one left but our group of Ward Four people including Mrs. Pilling and Mrs. Everett, and the Ward Two people, still enjoying themselves, playing bowls with the men now, Hilary and Carol receiving close instruction in the art of placing the bias. And who was that turning somersaults? Why, it was Mrs. Shaw, over and over and dancing with her dress up.

We patients from Ward Four looked horrified, and the nurse said, "It's a wonder they let people like that come out and mix." I think we murmured agreement. Pulling up our coat collars against the head wind (our own coats, not crumpled ward models with out-of-date fur collars and nipped-in-waists), we turned from the scenes of abandon provoked inexplicably by the mere opening of a bowling season, and walked, with our Ward Four dignity, down the hill towards the hospital.

We? I stayed behind. I had full parole. I was going home soon because my people would agree to "have me." I stayed for a formal and guilty hello and good-bye to the patients I knew, and went by myself down past the lupines and the wattle and the gorse, and past the dreary ward where, because it was too cold for them to be outside, the men, some still in their pajama coats, sat in the dining room staring at the wooden tables, not knowing or caring how to use up the hours until teatime and bedtime and tomorrow.

I looked away from them and tried not to think of them

and repeated to myself what one of the nurses had told me, "when you leave hospital you must forget all you have ever seen, put it out of your mind completely as if it never happened, and go and live a normal life in the outside world."

And by what I have written in this document you will see, won't you, that I have obeyed her?